Lyle, Lyle, Crocodile™

Lyle, Lyle, Crocodile ™

NOW A MAJOR MOTION PICTURE

ADAPTED BY
CATHERINE HAPKA

BASED ON THE
LYLE, LYLE, CROCODILE BOOKS
BY
BERNARD WABER

CLARION BOOKS
An Imprint of HarperCollinsPublishers

For Bernard Waber
With gratitude to Paulis Waber

Clarion Books is an imprint of HarperCollins Publishers.
Lyle, Lyle, Crocodile
TM & © 2022 Columbia Pictures Industries, Inc. All Rights Reserved.
Printed in the United States of America. No part of this book may be used or reproduced in
any manner whatsoever without written permission except in the case of brief quotations
embodied in critical articles and reviews. For information address HarperCollins Children's
Books, a division of HarperCollins Publishers, 195 Broadway, New York, NY 10007.
www.harpercollinschildrens.com

ISBN 978-0-35-875543-2

Typography by Stephanie Hays
22 23 24 25 26 PC/LSCH 10 9 8 7 6 5 4 3 2 1
❖
First Edition

Lyle, Lyle, Crocodile ™

It was a busy lunch hour in the famous New York City hotel's kitchen. Saucepans clattered. The head chef shouted. Cooks chopped, stirred, and sautéed for all they were worth. Tantalizing aromas filled the air. Waitstaff ran in and out of the kitchen carrying trays laden with sumptuous cuisine.

In the background, unnoticed by anyone, a shadowy figure stood in the doorway waiting for his moment.

Nobody paid any attention as the figure threaded his way through the kitchen. Nor did they notice him select a succulent shrimp from a waiting tray or skillfully swipe an elevator key card from a distracted chef. Not a soul caught sight of the mysterious visitor deftly hoisting a covered food tray to one shoulder, entering the elevator with a flourish.

Moments later the elevator doors swished open several floors above the kitchen, revealing the dashing figure of one Hector P. Valenti, self-proclaimed star of stage and screen, who stepped out of the elevator as confidently as if he owned the entire hotel. "Compliments of the house. It's delicious!" he exclaimed, depositing the tray in front of the security check-in guard, who was so startled he failed to stop Hector from rushing by. When he reached a corridor, Hector's sharp eyes swept over the posters plastering the walls—

SHOW US
WHAT
YOU GOT!

they proclaimed.

Hector smiled. He planned to do exactly that!

Hector confidently emerged through another doorway and found himself at the front of the long, long, loooooong line of people waiting to audition for the country's mo[...]

He didn't seem to n[...]

ignored ventriloquis[...]

paid no heed to come[...]

bands.

Without giving [...]

thought, Hector adj[...]

straight for the audi[...]

placed smoke plume to easily sidestep a second security guard and reappeared directly in front of the producers.

"Next!" a stage manager called, sounding bored.

Hector's eyes lit up. He straightened his shoulders. It was time for him to shine!

The show's producer looked just as bored as the stage manager. An even more bored-looking intern aimed a video camera at Hector.

The stage manager finally looked up. "Oh, no," he moaned. "Not again! We told you last time, Hector—no more!"

Hector swept into an extravagant bow. "That was just my song and dance routine," he insisted,

roducer his most charming smile.
ct will blow your minds! Prepare your-
r the *dance of a thousand pigeons*!"

Hector spun around, dizzyingly fast, and threw open his cape. There, in the folds of his clothing, were a few fluttering pigeons, doing their best to take their cue. Hector's confidence flickered, but he pressed on, removing his top hat with a flourish to allow one last pigeon to take flight.

★

THUMP!

Less than three minutes later, Hector landed on a hot, dirty, and very hard sidewalk in Times Square. Feathers drifted around him as his pigeons flapped off to freedom.

One of the security guards who had just thrown him out of the hotel gave him a sympathetic look. "Seriously, dude, ditch the birds," the guard advised. "You've got to find something we haven't seen before, because whatever that was ain't working."

The guard went back inside, slamming the

4

door behind him. To Hector, it felt like someone slamming the door on his dreams.

He climbed to his feet and limped off aimlessly down the street. He used the few remaining dollars in his pocket to buy a shish kabob from a street vendor, only to find it had gone cold. He ate it—that was the least of his worries—and crossed the street to drop his kabob stick into the nearest trash. Preoccupied with the day's disappointments, Hector almost missed seeing a store he'd never noticed before. It was tucked back along a grubby alley in a building that had seen better days. The sign read:

EDDIE'S
EXOTIC ANIMALS

Hector's shoulders straightened. He almost smiled. Then he pushed in through the door.

"I'm looking for something unusual but cute," he told the man behind the counter. "Really cute.

And affordable. And it has to fit under my hat while I'm dancing."

The man shrugged. "We got a special on bird-eating spiders."

Hector sighed. "Okay, let's try this again. . . ."

"Boa constrictor?" the man suggested. "Vampire bat?"

Suddenly, Hector didn't have the strength to explain to this man what the word "cute" meant. He was too tired. Tired of waiting for his luck to change. Tired of trying to convince the world that he was meant to be a star. Tired of scrounging for the smallest break when offers for his remarkable talents should be pouring in. He caught a glimpse of his reflection in the cash register—the reflection of a broken man who'd finally run out of luck, of optimism, of hope.

The counterman didn't notice Hector's rapidly deflating mood. "Wait," he said, his dull expression brightening slightly. "I might have a lemur in the back."

He disappeared, leaving Hector alone with a dozen or so listless animals. The only sound to be heard was an incongruously lively Latin tune on the radio. Hector turned to leave.

But then he stopped. Was that . . . *singing* coming from one of the cages? He blinked, listening more closely. The voice was melodious. Lilting. Captivating. Absolutely fantastic!

Hector followed the entrancing sound to the farthest corner of the shop. The singing seemed to be coming from a stack of cages there, and when he pushed past them he finally found the source: it was the tiniest baby crocodile he'd ever seen!

The little creature stood on its hind legs, barely a foot tall. Its miniature hips twitched as it sang along to the radio. There was a metal sign on its cage, so old that most of the letters had worn away. All Hector could make out was something that looked like

LYLE

Hector could barely breathe as his dreams came rushing back all at once.

"A singing *crocodile*!" he exclaimed. "Hector P. Valenti, at your service."

A short while later, a taxi turned onto an uptown street and stopped in front of an imposing brownstone. Hector slid out of the back, and little Lyle the crocodile jumped out after him.

For a moment Lyle just stood there gazing up in wonder at the house on East 88th Street. It towered over him, still exuding much of the grand beauty it had possessed when first built many years earlier, although by now paint was fading, bricks were crumbling, and an odd smell wafted from the direction of the trash cans under the stairs. Little Lyle didn't really notice any of that, though. He had never seen such an amazing place! It was majestic. Compared to his cage at the shop, it seemed like a palace!

He looked up at the man who had rescued

him from that sad shop. Hector smiled and swept his hand toward the house. "We're a family now. Welcome home!" he exclaimed.

Hector pulled out an ornate key adorned with a fancy tassel and turned the lock. Lyle hopped up the steps, each of which was nearly as tall as he was, and eagerly followed his new friend through the door.

There were many more steps inside the house. But Lyle didn't mind the climb, not one bit. It felt good to move around after being stuck in such a small area for so long.

Finally, he and Hector emerged into the house's attic. It was a bit dim, dusty, and drafty, but also surprisingly high-ceilinged and spacious. A large window opened onto the fire escape— and a breathtaking view of an endless sea of city rooftops. It was nearing dusk, and a cool breeze drifted in through the open window. Lyle shivered, partly from excitement, but mostly because it was chilly up there.

Hector cracked his knuckles and sat down at

an ancient piano. He hit middle C, then glanced over at Lyle with an encouraging smile.

Lyle smiled back. Hector looked happy, which made him feel happy, too.

Hector hit the note again. And again. Lyle cocked his head curiously, as he'd never before heard a song with only one note repeated over and over. Then again, he knew there were lots of things he'd never had the chance to experience while stuck in that shop. Now, perhaps, that was all about to change!

Hector cleared his throat dramatically. Even though he was very young, Lyle was also quite clever, and he was already figuring out that Hector did just about everything dramatically. Suddenly the man began to sing: "La, la, la, la, la, la, *laaaaa*!"

Lyle hardly heard him. He was shivering harder now. It was much too cold up here! While he didn't miss anything else about the shop, he was really starting to miss the heat lamp over his cage. He curled up into a ball, then let out a loud sneeze.

Hector abruptly stopped singing. "Wait—here you go," he exclaimed, jumping up and closing the window.

Then he removed his scarf and wrapped it around Lyle like a blanket. Lyle gazed up at him with a weak smile, more grateful than ever for his wonderful new friend. First, Hector had whisked him away from that terrible shop, and now he was making him feel cozy and more comfortable than he could remember ever being before in all his young life.

Hector smiled back. "Now listen to me," he began.

Lyle hardly heard him. He felt so contented that his eyes fluttered shut and his mind drifted away on a soft, warm cloud of happiness as the excitement of the day caught up with him—not to mention the exertion of climbing all those stairs. . . .

He was almost asleep when he heard Hector start playing the piano again. Hector had begun singing a loud and boisterous song. Yet beneath the surface Lyle detected hints of something more.

His new friend's voice sounded sad.

Lyle opened one eye. Why did Hector sound so dejected, especially on such an exciting day? He wasn't sure. But he knew one thing—the song he was playing was fantastic! Lyle loved music—all kinds. Listening to the radio, dancing and singing along to the tunes he'd heard, had been the only good thing about being in that shop. Now Hector's song filled his entire tiny body with light and joy.

"*La, la, la, la,*" he sang along, his beautiful voice filling the dusty attic with light and joy as well.

Hector turned and stared at him. Then that selfsame light and joy grabbed him, too. He grinned and started playing again, a little faster this time.

Lyle jumped up beside Hector, the music flowing through him from the tip of his tiny snout to the end of his little tail. They sang together, throwing themselves into the music, heart and soul, their voices harmonizing perfectly. Lyle danced along with the beat, and after a moment Hector leaped to his feet and danced, too, his fingers still flying over the keys.

It was the most fun Lyle had had in . . . well, maybe forever. And the best part? He could tell that Hector was just as happy as he was. Lyle felt like the luckiest crocodile on the planet. Somehow, in this vast, bustling city, he'd found—or, more accurately, been found *by*—something very special.

A best friend.

3

The next day, Hector left Lyle at home and went out to start making his dreams come true. Beyond Broadway—no, beyond off-Broadway—okay, way beyond off-*off*-Broadway—there was a little theater called the Coney Island Coronet. The owner, Cy, looked dubiously at a poster Hector had mocked up that morning. It featured Hector and Lyle in matching tuxedos.

"If you want the theater, it's ten thousand a night," Cy said. "In cash."

Hector gulped. "Cash may be a challenge." That was putting it mildly—he was flat broke. But he couldn't let that stop him, not when success was so close he could almost taste it. He had to find a way to make this work, no matter what it took.

He slid a hand into his pocket and pulled out the tasseled key, staring at it for a long moment.

The house on East 88th Street was the only valuable thing he owned in the world. It had been in his family for generations. Was he really willing to risk losing it?

Then again, it wasn't much of a risk once he stopped to think about it. After all, nobody had ever seen *anything* like Lyle before. When word got out, he and Lyle would be fighting off offers and swimming in cash. Because Lyle wasn't just another animal act or card trick. The kid could *sing*!

And so Hector nodded, knowing there was no other way. He had to take this shot.

"I have something far more valuable than mere cash . . . ," he told Cy, holding out the key.

Once the deal was struck, Hector knew he had work to do. He hurried home and got started.

He and Lyle rehearsed. They sang. They tap-danced. They did it all over again.

Lyle was everything Hector had hoped for and more. His dancing was almost as good as his singing. And his singing—well, it was nothing short of spectacular!

As the days passed before their big show, Lyle grew—and not only as an artist. Soon he was nearly three feet tall. He no longer fit under Hector's hat, but that didn't matter. Their performance would be way beyond any silly rabbit-in-a-hat trick. Or even pigeons-in-a-coat. Nobody had ever seen anything like a singing, dancing crocodile before. Nobody! They were going to be superstars!

Hector was so busy he hardly had time to breathe. He had music to practice, choreography to create, posters to distribute all over the city, and even a crocodile-size tuxedo to design and sew. But he made sure Lyle had plenty of time to relax and stay focused between rehearsals. Hector brought him sumptuous meals, soon realizing that Lyle's favorite dish was imported caviar. He filled the brownstone's old claw-foot tub with lavender bubbles so Lyle could spend hours soaking away the tensions of each hectic day. In short, he did everything he could to guarantee that their debut would be a smashing success!

Finally, the big day arrived. Posters covered the walls of the Coney Island Coronet, proclaiming:

One Man!
One Crocodile!
A Thousand
Songs!

The place was packed—every ticket had sold, and every seat was taken! Hector tiptoed onstage and peeked out between the curtains at the audience, thrilled with the turnout. *Finally!* he thought. *A crowd to match my enormous talent!*

Despite all their preparations, Lyle seemed a little nervous. Hector reminded Lyle to smile as they warmed up. He was upbeat. Encouraging! Nothing could ruin their plans. Stardom was their destiny.

When the orchestra struck the opening chords of their first number, they walked together onto the stage. Hector took a deep breath, offering a quick prayer to the gods of musical theater as he prepared to face his fate.

He smiled at Lyle, caught the hat a stagehand tossed him, and struck a pose. When the curtain went up, he strode forward and started to sing their opening number. It sounded fantastic!

But wait—something was missing. . . .

Glancing around, Hector realized that Lyle hadn't budged. He stared out at the crowd, eyes wide, not making a sound.

"Lyle!" Hector hissed. "You have to sing!"

But Lyle hardly heard him. He felt as if he were drowning in a sea of faces—SO MANY faces! Lyle hadn't known there were that many people in the entire *world*, and now they were all here, crowded into this little theater, staring . . .

directly . . .

at . . .

him!

This wasn't what he had expected. Not at all. He loved singing and dancing with Hector. But that was at home, just the two of them, having fun together. This was different. This was . . . *terrifying*! His gaze locked on a woman in the front row. She was gazing back at him. But why? Who was she? What was she thinking?

Lyle's limbs started to tremble. His eyes darted

to a man with a beard nearby, and then to another stranger, and another. . . .

The rest of him felt as if it were frozen in place, a block of ice. Some tiny part of his brain was aware that Hector was still dancing and singing, occasionally shooting meaningful glances at Lyle.

Lyle knew what his friend wanted. They had rehearsed this song so many times that the words, the notes, the dance steps were imprinted in Lyle's mind.

At least they *should* have been. Right here, right now, with all these strangers staring at him, Lyle's mind was a complete blank. He didn't remember a single word, a single note. His arms and legs and tail and body felt so stiff and heavy he wasn't sure how he'd ever been able to dance at all. He was barely able to figure out how to *breathe*.

Still, he knew his best friend was counting on him. And he would do anything to make Hector happy. So he reached deep down inside, opened his snout, and did his best to sing just the way they'd practiced. . . .

All that came out was a tiny crocodile *SQUEAK!*

The audience heard it. A few people started to snicker.

But many more people were booing. Some were already getting up to leave. Lyle froze again, overwhelmed by a creeping sense of utter failure and shame. . . .

In the wings, the theater owner saw what was happening. "Drop the curtain!" he shouted.

THUMP! The curtain slammed down, hiding Lyle and Hector from sight. On the other side of the thick velvet they could hear the audience gathering their things and shuffling up the aisles, some murmuring in confusion and others demanding their money back.

The angry stage manager cast a meaningful glare at Hector, who nodded solemnly in return.

★

That night, Hector rushed around the attic grabbing clothes and shoving them into a suitcase. Lyle watched anxiously. His ability to move had returned as soon as the curtain fell, and he'd soon stopped shaking. None of that made him feel much better, though. He knew he'd let Hector down. That was the last thing Lyle had ever, ever, *ever* wanted to do.

"What's that look for?" Hector said briskly and rather cheerfully, though Lyle couldn't help noticing that the man's smile didn't quite reach his eyes. "We've had a minor setback, nothing more. I'll hunt down fresh funds while you hold the fort here."

He finished packing and started toward the stairs. Then he turned, as if remembering one last thing. Grabbing a battered old portable music player, he handed it to Lyle, slipping the headphones over his ears before Lyle could react.

"And take this," Hector said. "It's got every song you'll ever need. The best companion there is."

Lyle didn't respond. He still didn't understand why his only friend was leaving. Then again, maybe it was his own fault. Hector had done so much for him—rescued him from that dingy shop, brought him here to this beautiful house, taught him to sing and dance, introduced him to fine caviar and bubble baths—and yet Lyle hadn't been able to do the one thing Hector had asked in return.

Still, he wished more than anything that Hector would change his mind and stay. But he couldn't talk to Hector except in song. And at that moment, Lyle felt far too heartbroken to imagine ever singing again.

Hector didn't seem to notice his friend's dejection as he pulled off his jaunty silk scarf and wrapped it around Lyle's neck. Then he gave a dramatic bow and wave.

"I'll be back in two shakes of a lamb's tail," he assured Lyle. "And remember—if anyone asks, tell them you're stuffed!"

With one last swish of his cape, he was gone.

Eighteen months later . . .

Time changes everything, even buildings made of brick and stone. Sometime during the long, sad months after Hector left, a $SOLD$ sign appeared in front of the house on East 88th Street. Soon it was followed by workers scrambling over every inch of the faded façade, restoring the elegant brownstone to much of its former glory.

And soon after that, a moving van pulled up to the curb, followed by a station wagon. The Primm family—Mr. Primm and Mrs. Primm, and their twelve-year-old son, Joshua—gazed out at the grand old house. They were a perfectly ordinary family. He had kind brown eyes. She exuded an air of quiet competence. Josh wore an expression of vague anxiety.

"Are we actually going to be living here?" Mrs. Primm asked in awe, her dark eyes gleaming with excitement.

Her husband checked the address on his phone, grinning gleefully. "I think we are!"

Josh leaned forward between his parents for a better look. He frowned and took a puff from his asthma inhaler.

"This is a *really* bad idea," he said, removing his supportive neck pillow.

Josh wasn't a fan of this move. For one thing, he'd had to leave behind his friends, his bedroom, his school . . . basically, everything he'd ever known. For another thing, this was *New York City*. Out of all the places in all the world, why had his parents decided to move *here*?

A million scary scenes from movies and TV shows set in New York flashed through Josh's mind. Except in his (sometimes overactive) imagination, his own terrified face appeared over that of every victim of monster or mobster, every casualty of comic book villain or disaster. He figured it was only a matter of time before his whole family was nothing but yet another grim statistic. . . .

Meanwhile, on the sidewalk in front of the brownstone's front steps, a woman named Carol was engaged in a rather testy discussion with a cranky-looking bearded man holding a beautiful, long-haired, silvery-white cat. "How can a tin-pot prep school own an asset of this brownstone's value and use it to house *teachers*? It's outrageous!" he declared.

"Mr. Grumps, please," Carol said with a sigh. "We can't keep having this conversation. The building was gifted to us by one of our alumni, as you well know. We are temporarily using it to house staff. I'm sorry your offer to buy it was refused, but there is really no more to say."

She turned away with an air of finality she hoped he would heed. Mr. Grumps rented the apartment on the ground floor of the brownstone, and Carol suspected he *enjoyed* making her life as difficult as possible. Just then she noticed the family climbing out of their car.

"You must be the Primms!" she exclaimed,

hurrying to greet them. "I'm so pleased to meet you. I'm Carol, from the Liberty Day School."

"Mr. Primm," Mr. Primm said, shaking Carol's hand.

"Your new Math Department chair," Mrs. Primm added proudly. "And this is our son, Josh."

Carol barely noticed the boy, who was the only member of the family still in the car. She was smiling admiringly at Mrs. Primm. "Can I just say what a huge fan of your cookbooks I am," she told her. "I can't wait to see what you do next."

Mrs. Primm cleared her throat. "I'm actually taking a break from all that to spend more time with Josh," she said. She smiled at her family.

Mr. Grumps stalked forward. Everything about him, from the top of his rapidly balding head to the whiskers of his gorgeously haughty cat, radiated hostility.

Carol gulped, realizing she had to get this over with. "Oh, and this is Mr. Grumps, your downstairs neighbor," she told the Primms.

"The local Neighborhood Association has established strict noise-abatement rules," Mr.

Grumps spat out. "Make sure you read them." He slapped a sheaf of pages into Mr. Primm's hand.

"Right," Mr. Primm said, seeming a bit overwhelmed by the hefty document. "We'll do that, won't we, darling?"

Meanwhile Josh finally got out of the car, staring at the cat in Mr. Grumps's arms. "That is the most beautiful cat I have ever seen," he said.

"Loretta is not a mere *cat*," Mr. Grumps said. "She's a silver-shaded Persian and has an extremely delicate constitution." He glared at the boy, putting extra emphasis on his next words: *"Do not feed her or let her out of the building."*

Carol decided it might be best to get the Primms safely inside before Mr. Grumps got really disagreeable. She ushered the family up the steps toward the main door.

"I will be watching them!" Mr. Grumps called after her. "And my *lawyers* will be watching them, too. One foot out of place and they will be *out!*"

SLAM! Carol was happy to shut the door—and shut out Mr. Grumps's incessant threats and complaints.

"I'd say his bark's worse than his bite," she told Mr. and Mrs. Primm with a wry smile, "but to be honest, his bite's pretty unpleasant, too."

"Amazing cat, though," Josh said. He turned to his parents with the first hint of a positive emotion he'd showed all day—namely, hope. "Can we have a pet?"

"Josh," his mother began, "we've talked about—"

"I know, I know," he cut her off, his shoulders slumping. "Allergies."

The Primms forgot about cats, and cranky neighbors, and everything else, as they finally took a look around their new home. It was *amazing*! Sure, the carpets might have seen better days. A few of the moldings had chips or missing bits. But enormous windows allowed the sun to flood the rooms with light. High ceilings and wide hallways made it feel more like a mansion than an ordinary house.

"FYI, there are a few leftovers from a previous owner in the attic," Carol said as they wandered through the main rooms. Mr. Primm looked up the stairs, noting that they ascended multiple floors, with this attic, he assumed, somewhere above all that. "Hopefully they won't get in your way. The floors are a little uneven, but three stories by the park is every New Yorker's dream." She smiled. "Welcome to your new home!"

★

That night, Mr. and Mrs. Primm lay in bed in their new house. Just outside their walls they heard an unfamiliar cacophony of city sounds. Horns beeped, busses rattled down the street, and late-night sounds of loud laughter and closing restaurants drifted upward. All wove together into a ceaseless urban concert they'd soon get used to. Tonight, it kept them awake as the enormity of the change in their lives began to sink in.

"New York City!" Mr. Primm murmured, his gaze wandering from the familiar objects around the room—the bedspread, his wife's favorite pajamas, the framed photo of him in his college wrestling singlet—back to the unfamiliar glow of the window.

"Did we just move . . . to *New York City*?" Mrs. Primm asked. She smiled, but then the smile faded. "Do you think Josh is going to be okay?" she added.

"Are you kidding?" her husband replied with a grin. "He's got his own floor up there—he's probably having the time of his life." He gave Mrs. Primm a kiss and tried to settle down to sleep.

★

At that same moment, Josh was *not* having the time of his life. He huddled under his blankets, wide-awake and twitching every time he heard a noise outside. And this being New York, also known as the city that never sleeps, there were a *lot* of noises outside.

"What was that?" Josh blurted out as he heard a distant, mournful wail.

His smart speaker glowed to life. *"Ambulance,"* its pleasant, female AI voice informed him.

Next Josh heard a strange screech echoing from the direction of the street. "What was that?" he yelped.

"Car tire," the AI replied.

After that came a terrible creaking. This time Josh was too terrified even to form the question, but the AI spoke up anyway.

"I have absolutely no idea what that was," it said.

Josh pulled the blanket even higher on his chin. The noise came again:

CRRREEEEEEEEEAK!

Josh's eyes moved up, up, up until he was staring at the shadowy ceiling of his new room. The creaking sound was coming from up there. Almost as if something was moving around in the attic just overhead.

He definitely couldn't sleep until he knew what was making that noise.

Very gingerly, Josh crawled out of bed. Tiptoeing as lightly as possible, he emerged into the hall and shone his phone's flashlight toward the steps disappearing up into the gloom of the old house's attic.

It took all the courage he had, but somehow Josh climbed those dark steps. He held his phone in one hand, its little beam feebly lighting his way.

In the attic, the phone's light hit a disco ball and cast a sparkling glow over the many dusty old boxes on the floor. There were tattered suitcases with a confusing assortment of items spilling out of them—fancy coats with elaborate cuffs; tubes of colorful, congealing stage makeup; a set of brightly painted juggling clubs; and much more that Josh was far too nervous to take in.

But he didn't see anything that might explain that creaking noise. At least not until he turned to go, and the phone's beam lit up the most . . .

. . . absolutely enormous . . .

. . . EYEBALL—staring straight at him!

Josh staggered back in surprise. Standing before him was a glass display cabinet. The eyeball belonged to the six-foot-tall, five-hundred-pound CROCODILE inside!

Josh moved his phone flashlight closer for a better look at the enormous animal, his eyes wandering from its scales and claws to the mouthful of razor-sharp teeth. He didn't know much about crocodiles—actually, he didn't know *anything* about crocodiles—but he couldn't help the impression that this one's jaws were arranged into what appeared to be an almost timid . . . smile?

Then Josh noticed the rather grubby silk scarf tied jauntily around the animal's neck. That was odd. Almost as odd as finding a big stuffed crocodile in his new home's attic.

Noticing a folded slip of paper pinned to the side of the cabinet, he grabbed it and scanned the short message penned in a distinctly ornate style:

Please be kind to my crocodile.
  He is the most gentle of creatures
and would not do harm to a flea.
  He is an artist.
  Perhaps he will perform for you.

Cordially,
Hector P. Valenti
(Star of Stage & Screen)

PS He is my most prized possession.
PPS His name is Lyle.

The most gentle of creatures? Josh looked at the crocodile towering over him in its display cabinet. It still seemed to be staring at him. Josh knew that wasn't possible, but it was unsettling nonetheless. He turned and hurried back down the stairs, careful not to look back.

Just in case.

★

The next morning, Mrs. Primm got up early. She wanted to start the family's first full day of their exciting new lives off right with a hearty, healthy breakfast. She threw herself into the task, humming happily as she worked. Just as she was setting the food out on the table, Mr. Primm rushed in.

"Tofu kale breakfast bowl, Swiss chard chickpea scramble, turmeric latte," Mrs. Primm announced proudly.

Her husband hardly seemed to hear her. He grabbed a slice of toast, jamming it into his mouth and holding it with his teeth as he shrugged on his coat.

"Wow, that looks amazing and so healthy," he said distractedly. "But I cannot be late—where's Josh? We have to go!"

"I'm taking Josh, remember?" Mrs. Primm said.

Mr. Primm looked relieved. He tried to kiss

her, but the toast got in the way.

"You've got this," Mrs. Primm assured him. "They're lucky to have you."

"I'm lucky to have *you*," Mr. Primm said gratefully, taking off for the door. "And tell Josh not to forget to sign up for wrestling!" he called over his shoulder as he left.

At that moment Josh sprinted in.

"We've got to go!" he exclaimed, sounding as frantic as his father.

"No, Josh," Mrs. Primm said soothingly. "We've got—"

He didn't even let her get as far as the tofu kale breakfast bowl.

"I checked it on the Safe Routes to School app," he said rapidly. "It's an eleven-minute ride on the subway from East Eighty-Sixth to our stop, plus a four-minute walk at this end and a seven-minute walk at the other. That's twenty-two minutes in total, assuming everything goes right. But if it doesn't go right—"

Finally Mrs. Primm managed to break into

his torrent of anxious words. "Josh!" she said. "There's time for breakfast."

But Josh didn't seem to hear as he dashed for the door. "I'll wait for you outside!" he called.

6

Josh hurried along East 88th Street, following the route on his app. He was totally focused on executing his plan to reach school on time.

"Keep up, Mom," he called, realizing she was falling behind. "All the way down to the end of the block—then we just have to cross this little avenue—"

He gasped, forgetting what he was about to say as he stepped around the corner—and into chaos. It was rush hour in Manhattan, which meant car horns blaring. Trucks careening past, rattling and wheezing. Taxis skidding around, changing lanes like they were in a video game. Fearless cyclists weaving their way through traffic.

And of course pedestrians. SO MANY pedestrians. More people than Josh had ever seen in one place before. All of them seemed to be in an enormous hurry.

"Wow," Josh breathed. "That's a lot of . . ."

His voice trailed off, and for a second he feared he might faint on the spot. It was too much. MUCH too much. Why had his parents decided to drag him away from his hometown, where he'd been perfectly happy, to this wild and frenetic place?

But they were here now, and there wasn't much choice but to plunge right in and follow the plan. Having a plan always made Josh feel better, so he took a deep breath, glanced at his phone, and turned toward the subway station just ahead.

Moments later, he and his mother struggled to stay together in the crowd as they made their way down the steps onto the subway platform. The underground air was thick with exhaust and . . . other smells. Ones Josh tried not to think too hard about.

He dodged a rushing woman, then a distracted-looking man. His elbow struck someone on his other side, but before he could get his mouth open to apologize, someone else brushed past, knocking his phone from his hand.

Josh winced as he heard it strike the concrete step. Sure enough, when he picked it up—a split second before someone stepped on it—the screen was cracked.

He sighed. *Yeah, this day is really off to a great start,* he thought with a grimace.

Finally he and his mother reached the platform. From deep in the tunnel came the roar of an approaching train. It exploded into the station with a draft that blew Josh's bangs straight up into the air, then screeched to a halt in front of them.

He glanced up at his mother, who looked a little overwhelmed herself, and thought back to all the times she'd taken his hand to help him through some difficult or scary new experience. He was twelve now, really too old for that sort of thing. But her hand was hovering there between them, and before he could stop himself, he grabbed it.

She looked down and smiled. He smiled back

and then, as the subway car's doors opened, they stepped onto the train together.

★

Josh's new middle school was as big and busy as New York City itself. He gave his mother a nervous wave and steeled himself to go walk in. At the last moment, he heard her yell, "Don't worry, you got this!" Josh, mortified by the giggles of the kids who overheard, was almost immediately sucked into a crush of students and swept inside.

At least the hallway smelled sort of familiar, much like middle schools everywhere. But the kids moved faster, talked louder, and seemed more self-assured than at his old school. Josh did his best to stay out of everyone's way as he walked down the hall.

Then he heard music. Nearby, a group of older kids were doing a complicated dance. They seemed so cool that Josh couldn't resist moving closer for a better look. As he did, he stepped right in front of a girl recording the performers on her phone.

"Seriously?" someone exclaimed as the girl with the phone let out a shout of dismay.

Suddenly many pairs of eyes were glaring at Josh. One of them belonged to a confident-looking girl who was the best dancer in the group as far as Josh could tell. She stormed over.

"Do you not see us filming right here?" she demanded.

Josh was mortified. "Sorry, sorry," he blurted out. "I was just . . . watching."

"Watch it on Sweep like everyone else," a boy said. Then he, the cool girl, and the rest turned and walked away.

★

After that, the school day was one long waking nightmare. He sat alone at lunch, next to trash cans that smelled almost as bad as they looked. Worse yet, his mother had filled his lunch box with stuff he barely recognized and certainly didn't want to eat. Healthy foods, like quinoa salad and a gluten-free cookie. Luckily, he had extra Bagel Bites in his backpack.

At wrestling tryouts Josh felt exposed and

uncomfortable in his slightly-too-snug singlet and padded helmet. It seemed like every other kid going out for the team took a turn body-slamming him, and he lost count of the number of times he was pinned.

It had been a lonely day for Josh. That night, he sat on his bed doing homework. Deciding to take a break, he reached for his phone and searched "how to make friends at school" but quickly switched to Sweep. He recognized the dancer in the newest video immediately.

It was the girl from school, the one with the confident look in her eyes. Apparently, her name was Trudy, and she was *amazing*. He couldn't stop watching as she performed a solo dance on his tiny screen, matching every beat of the hit song.

The music was loud, but not quite loud enough to totally hide a sound from the attic. For once, Josh was too distracted to worry about it. All he could think about was Trudy—how talented she was, how cool and generally amazing. He'd never met anyone like her before! It almost made him glad they'd moved here. *Almost.* He searched through Sweep, finding more and more of her videos.

Mrrrow!

Josh jumped, turning toward the open window. Framed against the dark sky he saw Loretta, the gorgeous Persian cat from downstairs. He smiled as she crouched down to lap at the saucer of milk he'd left out on the ledge for her. Maybe he couldn't have a pet of his own, but that didn't mean he couldn't get creative. . . .

"Loretta!" he murmured, "I knew you'd like the milk." He stepped over and scooped her into his arms. Her fur was like silk, her body warm, her eyes gleamed like jewels.

Meanwhile Sweep had looped back to Trudy's first video, the one with the catchy pop song. Settling himself on the bed with Loretta, Josh picked up his phone so she could watch the video, too. But before the song started to play, he heard the lyrics filtering down from the vent in his ceiling.

He froze, listening to the lilting voice singing

along in the attic. Was the house haunted? Could ghosts sing? He had no idea, and for a second he seriously considered diving under his covers and staying there until it stopped.

But then he took courage from Loretta's warm, purring body in his arms. With his new feline friend clutched to his chest, he headed for the stairs.

It wasn't easy to hold Loretta and also shine his phone's flashlight around the attic, but Josh managed. He saw the same boxes, the same suitcases, and of course, the same tall glass cabinet.

But wait—the cabinet wasn't the same after all.

It was *empty*!

Josh fell backward, scrambling away like an upside-down crab and losing his hold on Loretta. She landed on her feet where he dropped her, claws out, back arched, fur sticking straight up.

She was staring at something, an indistinct, very large silhouette in the darkness. Josh raised his flashlight with a shaky hand.

The crocodile was looking straight at him.

Now there was no mistaking it was alive. A deep, rumbling noise emerged from the creature's throat.

Josh wanted to scream. But all that came out was a terrified whimper.

He stared at the crocodile, his whole body shaking. Then, even consumed by fear, he noticed something.

The crocodile was shaking, too.

Lyle didn't notice the boy's terror. He was almost too scared to think. How had this happened? He'd been so quiet, so careful, spying on the brownstone's new tenants only when he was sure they weren't paying attention. He'd even pretended to be stuffed, just like Hector had told him to.

But he knew what his mistake had been: the music. It had been so long since he'd heard anything besides the songs in his scratchy old headphones that he hadn't been able to resist singing along with the catchy tune seeping up through the attic's floorboards from the room below. Now here he was, face-to-face with this young boy. What was he supposed to do? He wished Hector were here. . . .

MWORRR!

The one creature not completely frozen in fear was Loretta, who had climbed onto the top of the piano and seemed to be taking the situation into her own paws. She crouched briefly and then pounced on Lyle with every one of her razor-sharp claws extended like the alpha predator she believed she was.

As the cat flew toward him, a still-shaken Lyle opened his jaws wide in silent protest. And much to his—and Loretta's—surprise, she landed directly in his mouth.

GULP!

"NO!" Josh yelled.

★

Seeing the horrified look on Josh's face, Lyle could tell that he'd just made an even bigger mistake, and he had no idea what to do to fix it. "Run!" his instincts screamed, taking over for his still-frozen brain, and with a sudden swish of his tail, he dove out the open attic window and into the night.

8

"**O**hmigod-ohmigod-ohmigod," Josh exclaimed, racing over to grip the windowsill.

His eyes followed the crocodile—*Lyle*, his brain whispered to him, dredging up the name from that note—scuttling across the roof and down the fire escape, as agile as if he'd done it a million times before.

Then Josh heaved himself out the window onto the rooftop. He had to save Loretta!

He came to the edge of the roof and gulped. His fear of heights enveloped him in its clammy grip, making his legs quiver. Realizing his breath was starting to come in short, wheezing pants, he took a quick puff of his inhaler. Then he clambered down the fire escape, so desperate to get the cat back before it was too late that he hardly thought about how easy it would be to slip on the metal rungs. . . .

Below, Lyle heard the clattering of the fire escape as Josh descended, and looked back. The boy was chasing him! He couldn't believe this was happening. For all those long, lonely months he'd done as Hector said and stayed hidden, coming out only to find food. But now one song, one moment of carelessness, had changed everything, and Lyle had no idea what was going to happen next. He needed to find a new hiding place, one where he could stop and think about what to do. He leaped off the fire escape into the alleyway, toppling a line of trash cans. The resulting crash echoed off the walls.

Josh was still struggling down the last few rungs of the fire escape. "You have to give her back!" he called in the direction of the crashing sound. "You have no idea how much trouble I'll be in! *Please!*"

There was no response, so Josh jumped down from the fire escape and ran, following a scuttling noise and a barely visible shape in the shadows. He raced down the alley just in time to see Lyle collide with a clothesline, wet laundry briefly blocking his eyes. But that barely slowed Lyle down, and Josh followed, desperate to keep the runaway crocodile in view.

Within minutes Josh was again gasping for breath as he tried to keep up. He lost sight of Lyle for a moment at the end of the block, but then spotted him across the avenue just ahead, which was busy with traffic even at this late hour.

Josh didn't stop to think—he just ran. There was a cacophony of blaring horns and squealing brakes as vehicles swerved to avoid him. Shading his eyes against the angry glare of headlights, Josh put his head down and ran for his life, somehow emerging unscathed on the opposite side of the street.

He paused, gasping for breath, and looked around. There was no sign of Lyle. But an entirely different figure peeled itself out of the shadows and slunk toward him, eyes glinting with greed.

"You wanna give me your phone?" the man said threateningly. "Or am I going to have to take it from you?"

Josh froze. He was being mugged! He'd heard of such things, of course. He'd maybe even expected it to happen, living as he was now in a huge, terrifying city that the movies had taught him was full of crooks and countless other villains. But now that it was really happening, he was so scared that he couldn't move.

Nearby, Lyle heard the mugger, too. He paused and peered back at Josh, who looked utterly petrified.

Lyle stood there for a moment, unsure what to do. This could be his chance to get away while the boy was distracted! But somehow, he couldn't bring himself to leave him. Josh looked so small and scared—much the way Lyle himself felt before Hector rescued him, back when he was just a tiny crocodile all alone in the big city.

Hector had changed that feeling for him. Maybe now Lyle could change it for Josh.

He crept closer, still feeling uncertain. A low rumble built in his throat. Then he made the growl a little louder, and the man looked around in surprise. That was when Lyle really let loose:

ROOOOOOOOOOOOOOAAAARRRR!

Two things happened. First, the mugger ran away as fast as he could.

Second, Loretta leaped out of Lyle's mouth, right into Josh's arms!

Josh was so relieved that all he could do was grin and hug the cat tightly, her soft, slightly damp fur tickling his face.

He caught Lyle's eye. The crocodile stared back, looking oddly sheepish.

"That," Josh declared, his grin stretching even wider, "was totally *awesome!*"

Lyle's eyes remained fixed on Josh. Neither moved. Then a hint of a smile tipped the edges of the crocodile's mouth.

Josh clutched Loretta to his chest. He had rescued her! And Lyle—despite that amazing roar, maybe he *was* a gentle creature after all. He almost seemed . . . *shy.* Relieved, Josh glanced up and down the gloomy nighttime street. He gulped as he realized that nothing around him looked familiar. Before Lyle could slip away, Josh stopped him. "Wait," he said. "You've got to show me how to get back!"

The following morning, at the house on East 88th Street, Mrs. Primm was busy unloading a cardboard box they hadn't yet gotten around to unpacking. It was filled with food they'd brought from their last house, most of which she was putting away in the kitchen cabinets.

Mr. Primm walked in and peered into the box. His eyes lit up, and he grabbed a box of chocolate-covered cherries, popping several into his mouth.

"Those are horrible," Mrs. Primm protested. "Don't eat those!"

Mr. Primm stared at her. "What are you talking about?" he asked. "You love these things. You baked your famous cake with them and even made us put them on our wedding cake!"

"I know, but I finally looked up what's in them." Mrs. Primm shuddered. "They're filled with corn syrup and hydrogenated palm oil. Throw them out!"

Mr. Primm moved his arm over the trash can and sighed. Mrs. Primm wasn't fooled for a second.

"Seriously," she said with a laugh. "In the garbage—outside!"

With an even bigger sigh, Mr. Primm allowed his wife to add an open box of powdered sugar to the chocolate-covered cherries in his hands. He headed outside and down the steps toward the trash cans he'd seen tucked away in the lower entryway.

He was about to drop the sweet delights into one of the cans, when the lower-floor apartment door flew open. Mr. Grumps stalked out.

"Those are *my* trash cans, not yours," he snarled. "Yours are in the back." He started to turn away, then stopped. "And *someone* has been feeding my cat. I want to know *who*!"

Mr. Primm blinked. "Your . . ."

"Do you have any idea how dangerous irritable bowel syndrome can be in a cat as valuable as Loretta?" Mr. Grumps snapped. "If I catch you or your wife or your horrible son so much as looking at her . . ."

"What?" Mr. Primm exclaimed, startled out of his usual politeness. "Whoa, hold on one minute!"

But he backed down under the malevolent force of the neighbor's glare. "Do I make myself clear?" Mr. Grumps demanded. "Oh, and please," he continued sarcastically, "use more of the hot water. There's plenty to go around."

"Yes, yes," Mr. Primm said, meekly turning away.

★

Josh was supposed to be getting ready for school, but instead was in the attic with his new friend. Lyle looked sleepy—crocodiles are mostly nocturnal, after all—but Josh didn't really notice. He chattered nonstop at him: "I heard you turn on the heater—do you need a blanket or pillow? Hot water bottle? Also, I brought you a ball to play with."

He rolled a giant exercise ball toward Lyle, who stared at it drowsily. Then he held up an old belt that he figured was big enough to fit around Lyle's neck as a collar.

"I put my number on this in case you get lost," he said. "Do you want to put it on?"

Lyle didn't respond. But his narrowed eyes and turned head gave Josh his answer: that was not going to happen.

"Right," Josh said. "Maybe later. Oh—and this is my plus-four strength card."

He carefully held out his favorite collector's card. Lyle took it and stared at it uncertainly.

"It's the most valuable card in my deck," Josh explained. "I want you to have it."

Just then his mother's voice rang out from downstairs: "JOSH! WHERE ARE YOU?"

"I've got to go," Josh said. "But I'll be back after three." He grinned, hardly able to stop staring at Lyle. "An actual pet!" he exclaimed, and then he was gone.

★

"Wait!" Mrs. Primm called as Josh disappeared out the back door. "Where are you going?"

"I'm taking a shortcut!" Josh tossed back over his shoulder.

He cut down the alley, leaping onto a wall between buildings—the same one he and Lyle had traversed the night before. His mother burst out of the house just in time to see him.

"Josh, wait!" she cried, sounding horrified.

Josh hardly heard her. He parkoured his way down the block and onto the avenue. By the time his mother reached the subway, her phone open to an app that tracked Josh's location, he was leaning against the wall waiting for her.

"What's up?" he asked with a grin.

They headed down the steps. Moments later, a subway train thundered to a stop in front of them. Josh jumped aboard as soon as the doors opened, holding up a hand to stop his mother from following.

"Don't worry, I got this," he said. "I'll see you after school."

When she returned home, Mrs. Primm went up to her bedroom, still trying to process her son's sudden transformation. Sweet, timid Josh, with his fears and eccentricities, was acting like a totally different boy!

She tried a half-hearted workout on her rowing machine, but that lasted only a minute or two. It turned out, she couldn't row her worries away. Distracted, she checked her phone and saw a notification from her photo app: JOSH OVER THE YEARS. The image below showed her and Josh when he was just five years old.

She clicked on it. More photos appeared, then a video of the two of them playing together at the park near their old home. In the video, she spun a giggling little Josh around and around, singing him the old James Taylor song "How Sweet It Is (To Be Loved by You)." She watched and listened for a moment, amazed by the carefree joy in her own voice as the Mrs. Primm from the video sang the familiar lyrics.

Next was a video of a decadent cake, decorated with the family's favorite chocolate-covered cherries. Mr. Primm's voice could be heard from behind the camera: "Honey, it's perfect. That cake is going to make you famous."

She scrolled again, and this time came upon a video from her wedding to Mr. Primm. The two of them were laughing with friends, slicing their wedding cake together as everyone applauded. Yes, the same cake—homemade and decorated with their favorite chocolate-covered cherries.

Then the video cut away to the happy couple during their first dance. That James Taylor song was playing. Mrs. Primm's eyes filled with tears. . . .

★

Just above Mrs. Primm, a completely different type of eye peered down through a vent in the ceiling. It was Lyle. The music had roused him from his slumber.

He watched as Mrs. Primm leaned over the video. The camera zeroed in on the dance just as Mr. Primm swung his new bride around. Three-year-old Josh appeared, laughing as he danced along with them, his arms wrapped around each of their legs.

Lyle cocked his head, noticing the woman's wistful expression. . . .

★

Mrs. Primm grabbed a tissue from the box. She blew her nose, took a few deep breaths, then turned to leave the bedroom.

She stopped short. A bag of chocolate-covered cherries was sitting in the doorway!

Where did those come from? she wondered, picking them up. She was sure they hadn't been there a moment ago.

Or was she? She'd had a lot on her mind lately. It wouldn't be surprising if she were missing things. In any case, reminders of happier times *and* extra sugar were exactly what she *didn't* need.

She headed into the kitchen and dropped the chocolate-covered cherries in the trash.

★

During Josh's free period that day, he went to the library and pulled out every book they had about crocodiles. He sat down at a table and started reading through them, learning everything he could about his new pet.

"Hey, Animal Planet," a voice said as he was deep in a description of crocodiles' excellent night vision.

He looked up. It was Trudy—the girl from the dance videos.

"What's with all the books?" she asked.

"You . . ." He gulped. "You won't believe me."

Trudy stared at him. Josh suspected she wasn't a girl who took no for an answer very often.

"I just got a pet," he said. "Um, a pet crocodile. I'm trying to learn how to take care of him."

Trudy snorted. *"Nobody* has a pet crocodile."

Josh shrugged. "Told you you wouldn't believe me."

"And *absolutely nobody* has a pet crocodile in the city," Trudy went on. "My dad had to do free dental work for the mayor just to get my pet rattlesnake allowed in our building. A crocodile would be a *lifetime* of free cleanings!"

She turned to go. Josh cleared his throat. "I saw you . . . on Sweep," he blurted out.

She looked back. Josh felt his face turning red. How could he possibly explain how amazing he thought she was?

"It was," he stammered. "I mean," he burbled. "I've never . . . ," he tried.

Then he gave up and jumped to his feet. His arms flailed and his legs bounced around wildly as he attempted one of her coolest dance moves.

Trudy didn't say a word. But her stare said it all.

Finally she spoke: "You're kind of a weirdo, aren't you?"

With a hint of a smile, she was gone. Josh just stood there, wishing the ground would swallow him up. It could happen—he'd read several articles about sinkholes that had given him nightmares for weeks. . . .

PING!

It was his phone. When he glanced at the notification on the screen, his eyes widened and his face stretched into a huge smile. Trudy wanted to be friends on Sweep!

★

That night, Mrs. Primm stared at the ceiling above the bed. Her husband was sitting up beside her, reading by the soft glow of his booklight.

"Every parenting book and blog I've read," Mrs. Primm said. "They try to prepare you for this, but I still feel bad about it."

Mr. Primm marked his place in his book and glanced over. "About what?"

"Josh, growing up," Mrs. Primm replied with a sigh. She didn't notice movement behind the heating vent, or the huge eye peering out at them. "I should be happy about it, but I wish I didn't feel so left out."

Mr. Primm didn't see the eye, either. "Hey, you're a huge part of his life and an amazing mother," he said earnestly. "We were lost until you found us!" He pulled his wife in for a kiss.

Mrs. Primm kissed him back. But her heart wasn't in it. No matter what anyone said, she could feel Josh slipping away.

Though Mrs. Primm worried about him slipping away, his parents believed Josh was safely tucked up in bed that night. But they were wrong.

At that moment, he was racing down a darkened alley, a complacent Loretta tucked in his sweater, trying, again, to keep up with Lyle. Where was his new friend leading him now? This time, Lyle didn't try to outrun Josh. In fact, he stopped abruptly, stretched out his large claw, and brought Josh to a halt with a surprised *Oof.*

Josh struggled to catch his breath while Lyle turned his attention back to a door halfway down the alley. It swung open, emitting a burst of bright light, steam, and indescribable smells. A man emerged with several bulging trash bags, which he slung into a nearby dumpster without once looking around to spot the boy and crocodile watching him.

As soon as the door closed again behind the worker, Lyle edged forward. . . .

★

Josh didn't think the night could get more surprising. But by the time he found himself on a flat, nondescript tar paper rooftop with Lyle and Loretta, he was forced to rethink that. There, the soft neon glow of the city illuminated the unusual sight of the huge crocodile delicately laying out a sumptuous feast. Over the last hour, Josh had watched, and sometimes helped, as Lyle collected discarded food not only from the hotel kitchen, but from a Chinese restaurant, a French bistro, and more.

When the food was all in place, the meal looked perfect. Lyle dove in, devouring it with delight. After a moment he paused and looked up. Loretta, who had peeked out of her hiding place in Josh's sweater, pulled her head back inside.

But Lyle wasn't looking at the cat. Watching Josh, he carefully pushed a savory puff pastry toward the boy.

Josh gulped. "Oh, no," he said apologetically. "I have sort of, um, quite a specific diet. Which is mostly Bagel Bites."

He even more carefully slid the pastry back toward Lyle. Lyle pushed it toward him again.

"See," Josh said, "I'm not sure that's going to taste anything like a—"

He stopped talking then, his eyes following the pastry as Lyle scooped it up and balanced it on the tip of his snout. Lyle then began to juggle several of the pastries, using his hands, feet, and nose. As Josh's mouth dropped open in astonishment, Lyle allowed one of the puff pastries to roll down the pointy spines of his tail, all the way to the tip. . . .

FLIP! Lyle gracefully flicked the pastry high into the air. It arced up, up, up . . . and then down, landing in Josh's wide-open mouth.

Before he quite realized it, Josh had chewed and swallowed the deliciously airy pastry. He blinked. "Wow," he said. "That's amazing! I've never had anything like that."

He licked his lips. He glanced down at the

repast spread out before him. And then he sat down and tucked in.

The food Lyle had chosen was delicious! There were beef empanadas studded with raisins and olives, half-emptied tins of caviar, chicken dumplings, pasta smothered in butter and cheese, bits of buttery lobster, savory ramen noodles, and sardines dripping with parsley and garlic. Josh tasted everything, passing morsels of his favorites to Loretta, who happily gobbled them down.

"I've never had a pet before," Josh commented as the cat licked butter from his fingers. "I've always wanted one, but my parents won't let me." He glanced up at Lyle, who had stopped eating and was looking intently at Josh. "Where are you from? My mom's family is from Taiwan. Well, she's actually my stepmom. My real mom died when I was two. Dad says I've got her nose."

Lyle listened, his kind eyes never leaving Josh's face. Josh found it was nice having someone to talk to.

"I'm twelve, by the way," he said. "I'm also double-jointed. And I can crack all my knuckles in one move." He studied the crocodile's knobby clawed hands uncertainly. "Do you have knuckles?"

Lyle didn't answer. Josh shrugged and went back to eating. Then he thought of another question.

"Is this where you always come to eat your dinner? All by yourself?" he asked Lyle. "I do that at school, too."

Lyle met Josh's eye—and smiled. There was a vent in the roof nearby. Just then the sound of a lively song poured out of it. Josh realized there must be a Broadway theater below. He looked over in surprise as Lyle sighed with pleasure. The crocodile's tail began flicking back and forth, keeping time with the music. Lyle walked to the edge of the rooftop and looked out over the lights of the city.

And then Lyle began to sing.

The crocodile's voice as a youngster had been lovely, sweet and clear. As an adult, it was glorious. His tone soared, the stirring lyrics and lilting melody coming to life as the music poured out of his throat.

Josh's jaw dropped as he listened. Then he smiled, clapping wildly as Lyle leaped onto a ledge, silhouetted by a neighboring theater's marquee. The bulky body of the crocodile turned light and airy as Lyle danced, spun, and turned handstands in perfect time with the music.

When the song ended, Josh cheered and clapped. He couldn't believe that he'd ever hated the whole idea of living in New York City. Because right now, with the moon rising over the East River and his two amazing new friends beside him, he couldn't imagine being anywhere else in the world.

★

The next morning, Mr. Grumps paced restlessly back and forth in his spotless apartment. The phone was clutched to his face, which was twisted into an expression of extreme displeasure.

"Yes, it's an emergency!" he barked into the phone. "The city must ban the use of double-wide strollers on sidewalks—"

He gathered his breath to continue, but the person on the other end of the line had apparently heard enough. Realizing he was speaking to a dial tone, Mr. Grumps scowled and began furiously dialing another number.

Then he stopped as a particular odor drifted into his nose. He blinked. He looked around. He gasped as his eyes took in the horrific sight of a pile of *feline excrement* right in the middle of his *extremely* valuable hand-knotted wool rug!

Mr. Grumps raced into the hallway—and stopped just short of stepping in another pile. A few steps farther lay another, with yet another beyond. . . .

At the far end of the hall, Loretta was stepping delicately into her litter box. Then she paused— just long enough to vomit up a whole shrimp.

Mr. Grumps clenched his fists, practically spitting with anger.

Oh, not at poor, delicate Loretta, of course. This wasn't *her* fault. She'd led a sheltered life and, while extremely intelligent for a cat, couldn't be counted upon to make sensible choices, which was why he had to baby her so.

But it was *someone's* fault. And whoever that someone was, was going to *pay*.

★

Cradling Loretta in his arms, Mr. Grumps stared at his laptop. He was watching the feed from the security cameras he'd just had installed—three of them, mounted all around the outside of the building. As he watched a pigeon flutter past one of the cameras, he smiled with satisfaction and stroked Loretta's silky fur.

"Perfect!" he cooed, tickling her whiskers.

No one would be putting anything nasty in his darling girl's tummy ever again—not if he had anything to say about it!

★

A little later, an alert sounded on the laptop in Mr. Grumps's apartment. He sprinted in from the bedroom and peered at the screen. Two of the cameras showed nothing unusual. On the third, all he could see was a fuzzy fog, almost as if a furry blanket was covering the camera lens. Then he heard a noise from behind the house.

He marched outside and stared around, failing to notice Josh and Lyle, who had just rushed eagerly off for another nighttime adventure. But he did see someone else—Loretta! She was curled in front of the security camera, batting it with her paw every time it moved.

He slumped and sighed. "Princess, *please* . . ."

The following morning, Mrs. Primm cracked
open Josh's bedroom door. "Time for school,
Josh," she said.

There was no response. Josh's bed was empty.

His mother looked around. "Josh?" she called.

Then she noticed an open door farther down
the hall—the one leading up to the attic. But what
would Josh be doing up there?

She crept up the stairs, wondering. In a shaft
of morning light, she saw Josh, fast asleep.

"Josh?" Mrs. Primm said again, her voice
coming out slightly strangled-sounding this time.

Because she'd just seen what Josh was using
as a pillow.

A full-size crocodile!

Lyle and Josh opened their eyes, blinking
against the light. Mrs. Primm stood staring for

another heartbeat. Then she lunged forward, grabbed Josh, and started dragging him down the stairs.

"Mom!" he blurted out. "Wait. Let me explain. . . ."

★

Lyle recognized the expression on Mrs. Primm's face: it was sheer terror.

With a flick of his tail, he jumped up and disappeared out the attic window. He had to cut them off before they got all the way downstairs. He had to show Josh's mother that she didn't need to be afraid of him! Luckily he was pretty sure he knew the perfect way to convince her. . . .

Mrs. Primm and Josh were almost at the bottom of the steps when a flash of green scales appeared in the hallway. They found themselves staring up at Lyle, who had just slithered back inside through the bathroom window. He stood upright, blocking their way.

"Mom," Josh said. "It's okay. He's real, I know. But he's not—"

He stopped short as Lyle opened his mouth—and started to sing. The words and melody sounded vaguely familiar to Josh. But he saw that his mother recognized it immediately.

Lyle finished the song and disappeared back out the window. Josh wasn't sure what had just happened. His mother looked shocked and confused, which wasn't how she normally looked at all.

Mrs. Primm left her son in his room getting dressed for school and stumbled downstairs, her mind feeling as if it were exploding. Had that crocodile—that CROCODILE!—really just serenaded her with her wedding song, the one she'd just heard in that video: "How Sweet It Is (To be Loved by You)"? She'd known New York would be an adventure, but nothing could have prepared her for anything like this!

★

By the time the two of them were outside and on their way to the subway, Josh could tell his mother still hadn't fully recovered. Once again, he tried to explain: "Mom, I swear to you, he's not dangerous," he said.

"He's a *crocodile*!" Mrs. Primm exclaimed.

"Okay, yes, wild crocodiles are dangerous. Yes, they can bite through bone. Yes, they have a taste for human flesh." He shrugged. "But Lyle's not like that. He wears a scarf!"

Mrs. Primm just stared at him for a moment. "I have to tell your father." She pulled out her phone.

"He'll have him taken away!" Josh exclaimed frantically. After finally getting a pet—one with no fur for him to be allergic to, even!—he couldn't let things end this way. He couldn't let anyone take Lyle from him. "Lyle is a good crocodile," he pleaded. "He's just lonely. Like I was. And he cares about me."

His mother stopped in the middle of the sidewalk and looked at him. The call to Mr. Primm had gone to voice mail, and she hung up without leaving a message.

"Do you understand how different things have

been since I met him?" Josh went on. "I made a *friend*, Mom. I feel like I *belong* here. Because of *Lyle*!"

"Josh—" Mrs. Primm began.

"You won't even see him!" Josh promised desperately. "He's nocturnal. And he can sing!"

Mrs. Primm's phone buzzed. It was Mr. Primm calling back.

She hesitated, gazing at her son. He gazed back.

"Just don't do anything until I get home tonight," he pleaded. "That's all I'm asking. Please . . ."

Mrs. Primm answered the phone. "Honey, did you call?" her husband asked.

Josh held his breath and shot her his best pleading, puppy dog eyes. He knew she'd never been able to resist that.

"Oh, I just . . . wanted to wish you a great day," she blurted into the phone before quickly hanging up. "I can't believe I just said that." His mother was flustered, it was true, but Josh let out a sigh of relief. He knew she'd agreed to only one day. But with Lyle's help, he was sure he could convince her to let his new friend stay—forever.

★

At the other end of the line and several blocks away at Liberty Day School, Mr. Primm was in the corridor hunched over his phone. "Thanks, I could use it," he said, not realizing his wife had already hung up. He shot a look toward his open classroom door. Inside, chaos reigned as usual.

He took a deep breath and straightened his shoulders, trying to look as confident as possible. Then he stepped into the uproar. Girls were shouting across the room, some with their feet up on the desks. Others played with their phones, oblivious to their teacher's arrival—or maybe just not caring.

"Everyone!" Mr. Primm said loudly. "Everyone, please—"

There was no discernible response from the students, and he sighed. After only two days, he was already used to being ignored.

Back on East 88th Street, Mrs. Primm pushed gingerly through the front door. The house was very still. There was no sign of the crocodile in any of the downstairs rooms.

Only one thing was different from when she'd left. The bag of chocolate-covered cherries was back, sitting in the middle of the rug.

Mrs. Primm frowned. *What kind of game is that creature playing?* she wondered uneasily as she scooped up the sugary treats and dumped them back into the trash.

Feeling an increasing sense of dread, she opened a closet and grabbed a broom, holding it in front of her like a weapon. Her heart leaped into her throat as she finally heard a sound:

SWISH, SWASH, SPLASH, SWOOSH!

It was coming from upstairs! She lifted the broom, eyes wide and heart pounding. The sound came again:

SWISH, SWASH, SPLASH, SWOOSH!

Wielding the broom, Mrs. Primm crept upstairs. Light was seeping out from beneath the bathroom door. She edged forward and pressed herself against the wall, broom raised, ready to attack.

SWISH, SWASH, SPLASH, SWOOSH!

Taking a deep breath, Mrs. Primm burst into the bathroom—and stopped short in surprise. The big claw-foot tub was almost overflowing with water and bubbles . . . and a giant crocodile!

Lyle had his headphones on, turned up loud enough for anyone nearby to recognize the lively Stevie Wonder song pouring out. He was singing along, his beautiful voice echoing off the bathroom tiles.

He loved bubble baths, and he'd soon discovered that there was plenty of time to fit one in while Mrs. Primm was taking Josh to school. He wasn't expecting today to be any different—until a loud gasp cut through the funky bassline flowing into his ears. Lyle's eyes flew open—Mrs. Primm was standing there staring at him!

He leaped to his feet, water dripping from his scales, and covered himself with his scarf. Mrs. Primm screamed. And Lyle, just as shocked by her as she was by him, screamed back. Mrs. Primm threw the broom at Lyle and dove for the door, practically falling into the hallway.

Horrified, Lyle jumped out of the tub, sending water cascading everywhere. He hadn't expected her home so soon. She already didn't like him—he had to find a way to win her over! But nothing he'd tried so far seemed to be working.

When he emerged from the bathroom, she was running down the stairs. Lyle leaped onto the banister, sliding down after her. He followed her into the kitchen, where she spun to face him. They stood there for a moment, staring at each other and breathing hard.

Keeping his gaze on Mrs. Primm, Lyle backed toward the trash bin, gently tipping it over with his tail. The chocolate-covered cherries spilled out, and he kicked them toward her.

Lyle wanted her to understand that she didn't have to worry—that he wanted to make her world sweeter, that she had no reason to be scared of him. That they could be friends, just like he was friends with Josh. Now that he had her attention, he figured the best way to show her was through music.

Lyle began to sing. His song was all about cooking without a recipe, stepping away from the boring and predictable, and creating something new and wild and wonderful.

Mrs. Primm still looked a little worried, a little confused, a little suspicious. But Lyle could tell that she was listening to him—and maybe to the song's message, too.

He danced around the kitchen. Taking inspiration from the words he was singing, he shimmied over to the stove to taste the fiber-packed oatmeal Mrs. Primm had made for breakfast, but immediately spit it out—yuck! It tasted like sawdust.

Lyle picked up the cookbook lying open nearby and glanced at it. He didn't like the look of the ingredients, so he tossed the book aside and started improvising, grabbing everything delicious he could find and tossing it into the pan.

Mrs. Primm looked alarmed. She chased after him, trying to stop him from turning her recipe into a muddled mess—not to mention her kitchen. Every time Lyle turned away, Mrs. Primm raced forward to tidy up spills or slam cabinets shut. But there was no stopping a crocodile on a mission. As Lyle stirred a few more ingredients into the bubbling pot, Mrs. Primm tilted her head, beginning to look . . . intrigued.

Lyle noticed her expression. He quickly scooped out a spoonful of his concoction and held it up to her nose.

Mrs. Primm's mind was in a tizzy. Part of her was horrified that there was a crocodile in her kitchen messing with her oatmeal. But another part was trying very hard not to give in the music, the dancing, the incredible sense of fun. . . . She stared at the spoon in front of her face.

After a beat, she leaned forward and took a sniff. Her eyes widened. Whatever that mess was—it smelled absolutely amazing!

She took a small, cautious bite. A riot of flavors exploded on her tongue. Her nose hadn't lied. The muddled mess . . . was *delicious*!

Mrs. Primm still couldn't quite believe this was happening. But when was the last time she'd let loose and had as much fun as Lyle was having right now? Her toes started to tap. Then her hips began to shimmy.

Lyle took Mrs. Primm by the arm, and she didn't resist as Lyle spun her around and swooped her into a deep dip, both their feet now dancing to the rhythm. A huge grin spread across her face as she gave in to the song, singing along with Lyle. When he danced over to the whiteboard where she had the entire family's schedule outlined down to the minute, she didn't hesitate before giving him a nod. He wiped the board clean, then looked at her.

She laughed and threw herself into the dance, grabbing a handful of sugar and tossing it into the pan.

★

When Josh let himself into the house after school, the first thing he heard was laughter coming from the kitchen.

He followed the happy sound and found his mother and Lyle in the formerly spotless kitchen, which was now an absolute disaster area—pans and baking tins littered every surface, a bag of flour spilled out on countertops, and chocolate-covered cherries were everywhere.

But Josh hardly noticed the mess. All he could focus on was his mother and Lyle. Together. Looking happy. Enjoying each other's company. Lyle had a chocolate-smeared spoon clutched in one clawed hand, while Mrs. Primm was laughing in a way Josh hadn't seen her laugh in a long time.

A smile spread across Josh's face. He wasn't quite sure what had happened while he was at school. But he didn't really care.

This was great!

For the next couple of days, life was much more cheerful in the house on East 88th Street—at least for Josh, his mother, and Lyle. Josh spent as much time as he could in the attic with his new friend. And while he was at school, Lyle came downstairs to spend time with Mrs. Primm. They sang, they danced, they cooked. Mrs. Primm took up painting again, creating charming portraits of the huge crocodile, who was happy to pose for her as long as she liked. Her days weren't as neatly organized as they had been before, but they were a lot more fun!

One afternoon Josh finally confessed to her about their nightly food-scavenging trips around the city. She absolutely forbade him from doing it again—unless she could come along. Mrs. Primm never would have imagined it could be so magical to sit atop a tar-paper roof at midnight, high above the buzzing glow of the city, gazing over an endless sea of rooftops and water towers. She dined on scraps of every heavenly gourmet food one could imagine, while right beside her a friendly crocodile gobbled down canapes, crepes, pad thai, and pancetta.

But the very best part for Mrs. Primm was watching Josh. He was willing to taste whatever Lyle found. He didn't necessarily like all of it—but he liked a lot of it. And his newly adventuresome palate wasn't limited to those nighttime feasts, either. He'd become much more willing to taste every meal she made for the family. She couldn't even remember the last time he'd asked for a Bagel Bite!

The only one in the house who wasn't happy was Mr. Primm, though the others scarcely noticed. But he noticed their change in mood, which made him feel like even more of a failure. Why was he the one member of the family who couldn't seem to fit in here? He was still struggling to find his balance at his new job. At night, he read books

The Primm family moves into the house on East 88th Street in New York City.

Their new home has bright windows, lots of space, and one BIG surprise . . .

Lyle, Lyle, Crocodile lives there, too!

At first, Josh has a hard time feeling at home in New York.

But in Lyle, Josh finds a best friend.

Lyle inspires Mrs. Primm to have more fun
and to look at things differently.

Even Mr. Primm is surprised by how much
he enjoys having Lyle in the house.

When Hector P. Valenti, star of stage and screen, arrives on their doorstep, the Primms learn more about Lyle.

Hector and Lyle used to perform together. Or, at least, they tried to. Lyle gets stage fright!

Life with the Primms and Hector is full of sweet surprises.

Lyle has never been happier!

Mr. Grumps, the Primms' neighbor, does not think a crocodile belongs on East 88th Street. He vows to send Lyle away!

With Josh by his side, Lyle finally gets the courage to sing for an audience.

Lovable Lyle sings his way right into their hearts!

Lyle gets to stay at the house on East 88th Street.
Right where he belongs.

about tapping one's inner strength, about winning respect, about becoming successful and powerful and assertive. But none of the books' advice helped him. His students continued to ignore him at best, disrespect him at worst, and by the time he walked out of school on Friday it felt like a narrow escape.

How was he going to force himself to return to that torture on Monday?

By Saturday morning, he still wasn't sure. He tromped downstairs, yawning and craving coffee. When he entered the kitchen, his wife was humming a cheerful song he didn't recognize. She and Josh were at the table eating.

But *what* were they eating? Mr. Primm blinked and rubbed his eyes, wondering if he was still asleep and dreaming.

"Pizza for breakfast?" he blurted out.

Josh opened a small container of something and dumped it onto his pizza slice. Mr. Primm took another step. Okay, now he was sure he had to be dreaming. Since when did his finicky son eat *caviar*?

BRRRRAAAAAAP! Josh burped loudly. "Excuse

me," he added, clearly trying not to laugh.

Mr. Primm glanced at his wife. He wasn't sure what he expected her to do about Josh's burp, but whatever it was, it wasn't what actually happened. *RRRRRRRRAAAAWWWWAAAAARRRRAAAAAWP!* she burped twice as loudly as Josh.

She and Josh burst out laughing. Mr. Primm just stared, completely lost. If this was a dream, he was ready to wake up now.

But it wasn't a dream. So he did his best to remain calm and act normal. Finally, after Josh disappeared upstairs and Mrs. Primm started cleaning up, humming cheerfully, he cleared his throat, unable to stay quiet any longer. He had to express the worry that had been plaguing him these past couple of days, even more so than the worry over his job.

"Darling . . . ," he began uncertainly, getting up to help with the dishes. He paused, trying to figure out the best way of putting his fears into words. "You've been so happy recently. . . ."

Mrs. Primm stopped and turned to face him. He could see that something in his tone had caught her attention, and he wanted to get this out before he lost his nerve.

"Which is great . . . and I wondered if maybe it wasn't because of me?" He went on, his voice coming out sounding strained. "Is there something . . . something you're not telling me?"

"Oh, sweet pea!" Mrs. Primm exclaimed.

But he couldn't stop now. Not until he knew. "Is there someone else?" he blurted out.

His wife grabbed his hands and gazed thoughtfully into his eyes. "Not exactly," she said.

★

Josh was scrolling through Sweep to see if Trudy had posted any new videos, when his mother walked into his bedroom. "It's time to tell your father," she announced.

"Time to tell your father what?" Josh's dad came in, too, looking confused.

Just then they all heard the toilet flushing across the hall. The bathroom door opened, and Lyle stepped out, drying his hands on a towel.

Oops, Josh thought.

★

Lyle stood frozen in place, every bit as terrified as Mr. Primm, who managed to recover enough to grab his family and drag them away.

"Get to our bedroom and lock the door!" he yelled.

"Darling . . . ," Mrs. Primm began soothingly.

But her husband didn't seem to hear her. His eyes were wild as he shot an incredulous look at Lyle. "I mean it!" he shouted. "I'm calling the police."

He pushed and shoved the two of them along the hall and into the main bedroom. Josh tried to resist.

"Daddy, it's okay!" he exclaimed.

Lyle leaped into action at the distress in his friend's voice. He raced down the hall, sliding through the bedroom door before Mr. Primm could slam it.

"It's not okay!" Mr. Primm shouted, backing away from Lyle with his family pressed behind him. "It's a CROCODILE!"

"That's what I thought, too," Mrs. Primm spoke up. "But he's not a normal crocodile."

"What are you *talking* about?" her husband cried.

Lyle swallowed hard. This looked bad. But he'd won over Josh. He'd won over Mrs. Primm. He had to find a way to win over Mr. Primm, too.

His gaze fell on the framed photo of Mr. Primm in his wrestling days. Then his eyes wandered to another frame hanging nearby, this one holding the very same singlet and whistle the younger Mr. Primm was wearing in the photo. It gave him an idea.

He turned and stepped up to Mr. Primm, copying his wrestling stance from the photo. He imagined himself wearing a singlet like the one in the picture, with a whistle hanging around his neck just like the younger Mr. Primm had.

The current-day Mr. Primm stared at him, looking more terrified than ever. "Um . . . ," he began.

Lyle pursed his lips and let out a piercing whistle. He stepped quickly toward Mr. Primm, waving his claws as if to say "come and get me!"

Mr. Primm was *not* interested in wrestling with a crocodile. He frantically scrambled back out into the hallway.

"Darling!" Mrs. Primm exclaimed, sounding concerned. She hurried out after him, followed by Josh.

Lyle was puzzled. He'd become friends with Mrs. Primm by joining her in something she loved—cooking. He'd only been trying to do the same with Mr. Primm. His face in that wrestling photo looked so happy, so proud. Why hadn't Lyle's gesture of friendship worked this time?

★

Mr. Primm rushed downstairs, waving his arms for Josh and Mrs. Primm to follow. "We have to get out of here!" he shouted frantically.

When Mr. Primm ripped open the front door, he stopped short. A man was standing there, fist raised as if about to knock. The other hand was using a flamboyantly long and colorful pocket square to mop his brow.

"May I wish you a good day, sir!" the man exclaimed.

Mr. Primm blinked. This was the oddest-looking

fellow he'd seen in some time. Was that an actual *cape* he was wearing?

As Mr. Primm stood there gawking, the man flipped off his hat, rolled it down his arm, caught it in his hand, and swept into an extravagantly old-fashioned bow.

"Hector P. Valenti, at your service," he declared. "Where should I put my bags?"

Mr. Primm stood rooted to the spot. After the morning he'd had, this was too much. His brain simply couldn't catch up to what was happening.

"I'm," he stammered. ". . . not . . . ," he added.

"Oh, dear," Hector said. "Didn't you know I was arriving?"

Mr. Primm was still lost. He looked at his wife as she joined him at the door.

A lifetime at the edges of show business had taught Hector not to wait for others to offer opportunities, but to make things happen for himself. He stepped forward, easing past them both and into the brownstone.

"While you call the school authorities, I'll make myself at home." Then he nodded toward the two huge, overstuffed suitcases he'd left sitting just outside. "Please, be my guest," he told Mr. Primm, hoping the man would take the hint and bring them inside. "The trip was a hard one, and I'd hate to put my back out the moment I . . ."

The words trailed off. He'd just spotted Lyle on the staircase.

Hector was a difficult man to surprise. But he could hardly believe what he was seeing. He stepped forward until they were eye to eye, sizing up his old friend. "Well, I'll be!" he exclaimed. "Look at the *size* of you!"

Lyle stared back, looking stunned. Then his expression shifted, though Hector couldn't quite read it. Moving slowly and deliberately, Lyle turned his back on Hector.

"Lyle?" Hector said.

Lyle heard him, but he didn't respond. He couldn't. He was too surprised, too confused, too overwhelmed by Hector returning just as suddenly as he'd left. How could he just walk in and say hello as if only a day had passed, instead of eighteen months that had felt like a lifetime?

Then, behind him, he heard Hector move. Lyle's hearing was as keen as that of any crocodile, and he could tell that the man had just taken a long, slow, sliding step to the right. A second later he clapped his hands.

A shiver ran through Lyle as he recognized the cue. He tried to resist, but his body responded in spite of himself. His clawed toe twitched. He slid one foot to the left and twitched his tail.

He turned and saw his old friend grinning with delight. Then Hector took another step, gave another clap.

Lyle mirrored the man's steps, clapping along as he performed their routine. Even after being apart for so long, their timing was perfect. Left, right, back, forth—the dance finally ended with Lyle sliding down the banister and landing in Hector's arms.

Hector beamed at the amazed Primms, awaiting their applause. He still had it!

Then his knees buckled. His back started to give out. He collapsed, buried beneath a dance partner that currently weighed several hundred pounds more than the last time they'd performed this particular number.

"Not quite as strong as I used to be," he said with a chuckle, extricating himself from beneath Lyle's scaly bulk.

★

It took a few phone calls from the privacy of the kitchen before the Primms could make any sense at all out of what was happening. Finally, Mrs. Primm spoke to someone at the school with knowledge of the mysterious Hector P. Valenti. "No one told us anything," she repeated into the phone, with a curious look at Mr. Primm. "Okay, thank you. Thank you." And with that, the call was over.

"Apparently, it used to be his family's brownstone," she announced, shooting a wary glance around and listening for signs of Hector approaching the kitchen. "He lost it in some sort of business deal or something. He's trying to mount a new show, and there's a clause that says he can stay here fifteen nights a year." She started sketching a crocodile, complete with bumps and ridges and a shy smile to soothe her nerves.

"What?! This cannot be happening," Mr. Primm said. "We've got a crocodile *and* David Copperfield living in our attic." He frowned as he noticed what she was doodling. "And can you please stop drawing him? It's . . . weird."

★

Hector's sudden appearance at their door didn't only affect the Primm family. That night, music, laughter, and creaking floorboards kept everyone in the brownstone awake.

That included Mr. Grumps, who lay in his bed, trying to sleep. But the noise was impossible to ignore. He ripped off his velvet eye mask and shook his fist at the ceiling.

"I hate you," he said.

On the bed beside him, Loretta peered out from beneath her matching velvet eye mask and yawned.

16

Sunday morning seemed a little quieter, at least at first. A bleary-eyed Mr. Primm stumbled down the hallway to the bathroom, hoping a hot shower would help make up for his lack of sleep.

He opened the door and immediately snapped wide-awake. Hector was in the shower, singing an old Motown tune as he scrubbed himself vigorously with Mr. Primm's washcloth. The room was a mess—wet towels were draped over every surface, clothes hung haphazardly from the shower rail, and toiletries were scattered everywhere.

Hector noticed Mr. Primm. "I bid you a fine good morrow, sir," he said cheerfully, grabbing his toupee off a Styrofoam stand and popping it onto his wet head.

Mr. Primm glared at him. He marched into the

room, grabbed his toothbrush and toothpaste, and headed back out again, thanking his lucky stars that the brownstone had more than one bathroom.

"If there's any breakfast, I'll take eggs. Any way you want to make them. But not scrambled. Or fried!" Hector called after him before launching back into his song.

★

Upstairs, Lyle was singing the same cheerful tune as he tidied the attic. Hector had made a mess of the place, but he didn't mind. Lyle danced over the old floorboards, gathering clothing and the odd piece of rubbish, making the place feel homey for Hector. It was wonderful to have his old friend back—especially after thinking Hector had abandoned him forever.

Lyle couldn't wait to see what came next.

The morning sun shone, bright and full of potential, on the front steps of the brownstone. Josh and his mother waited there, debating whether their "family day" adventure should take them to the museum or the zoo. Josh was surprised to see his father step past them dressed in his running gear and disappear down the block.

"Dad isn't coming?" Josh asked.

"Dad needs to let off some steam," his mother replied.

Josh nodded. "He doesn't really like Hector, does he?"

"Hector . . ." His mother paused, as if searching for exactly the right words. ". . . is a very colorful character."

As if on cue, the front door flew open to reveal the man himself. Hector was dressed from head to toe in bright blue and even brighter orange, with just a hint of green to set it off. Somehow he managed to look even more extravagant and outlandish than usual, even without his cape.

"I don't know about you," he declared, patting his stomach, "but I could eat a horse if you spread butter on it!"

Josh blinked. Suddenly he remembered a college football game he'd watched with his parents, and the color scheme clicked. "You're a Florida Gators fan?"

Hector snorted. "Don't be ridiculous." As Josh and Mrs. Primm stared at his clothes, he waved a hand dismissively. "Smoke and mirrors, my friend, smoke and mirrors! How else do you think Lyle can join us?"

The door creaked open again. This time Lyle tiptoed out, looking a bit nervous.

Josh stared at his friend. The huge crocodile was covered from head to toe in University of Florida Gators gear. A Gators vest stretched across his torso. A Gators cap was pulled down over his head. A Gators scarf hid most of his face and snout. He even wore a pair of Gators sunglasses! If you didn't look too closely, he almost could pass as a Florida Gators mascot.

Almost.

They set off down the block and turned onto the avenue. In New York City, not much attracts the attention of jaded urban pedestrians.

But Lyle did. People stopped, goggle-eyed, when he passed them. A toddler in a stroller pointed and cried out. A bicycle messenger was so distracted by Lyle that he almost steered straight into the side of a van.

"Do you really think this is safe?" Josh asked nervously.

"Who wants to be *safe*?" Hector exclaimed. "Safe is such a repellent little word! Expunge it from your mind. We are here to *live*! And living is a dangerous business."

"You're . . ." Mrs. Primm cleared her throat. "Er, not worried that some people might think he's a real crocodile?"

"Nothing could be of less importance than what other people think," Hector declared.

Another pedestrian craned her neck to stare as she hurried past. Hector tipped his hat to her.

"Let people stare," he told the Primms. "For once in their dreary lives they have something wonderful to look at." With that, he jutted out his chin, linked arms with Lyle, and strutted off down the sidewalk.

Josh and his mother traded a look. Then they both began to grin. *Why not go along with him?* Josh thought as he hurried after Hector and Lyle with his mother at his heels. *What's the worst that could happen?*

★

The rest of the day was wonderful. The four of them had ice cream for breakfast, with Hector grandly ordering half the menu. Lyle barely managed to squeeze around the table with them, and Josh couldn't help noticing the other patrons staring. But he tried not to let it bother him. Like Hector said, who cared what anyone thought?

When their ice cream arrived, the other customers stared again. But all they saw was Josh,

Mrs. Primm, and Hector scooping up small tastes of the frozen treats. So they turned away—and as soon as they did, Lyle wolfed down every bite of ice cream on the table.

Suddenly the crocodile's eyes widened. He gripped his head and moaned.

Josh grinned. "Brain freeze!" he shouted.

After Hector graciously accepted Mrs. Primm's offer to pick up the tab, the group headed out to explore. Hector suggested they take a stroll through Central Park, so they all crammed themselves into a taxi. Lyle didn't quite fit, but he was happy riding with his head sticking out the window.

When they reached the park, Mrs. Primm wanted to rent a surrey bike. It tipped a little bit toward the side Lyle was on, but they had fun nonetheless.

After that came a visit to a museum, some window-shopping, and lots of talk and laughter. By then Josh hardly noticed the stares. He was too busy having fun with his mother and, yes, even Hector, but especially with his best friend, Lyle.

It was a wonderful day.

That evening, Josh, Mrs. Primm, and Lyle were tired but happy. They sat in the living room of the brownstone playing board games while Hector rummaged in the kitchen for snacks.

This was the scene that greeted Mr. Primm when he walked in. After his long morning run, he'd spent the rest of the day running errands and just wandering around the neighborhood, trying to figure out where his life had gone so wrong. His job was terrible. There was a stranger living in his house, with an emphasis on *strange*. Worst of all, for some reason his beloved and normally quite sensible wife was opposed to that stranger removing the enormous crocodile that was *also*, somehow, living in his house.

None of it made sense. And he couldn't figure out what in the world to do about any of it.

His wife looked up with a smile when he entered. "Perfect timing," she sang out. "You can be on my team."

"Oh, no, I'm exhausted," Mr. Primm told her. "I'm going to take a shower."

"Hector says the hot water is out," Mrs. Primm warned.

"Sorry!" Hector called from the other room.

Mr. Primm grimaced. At least maybe this was one thing he could fix. . . .

He headed for the stairs. Behind him, he heard heavy footsteps and realized the crocodile was following him. But he did his best to ignore that as he made his way up to the attic.

When he got there, he stopped and stared at the boiler, trying to remember how such things worked. Behind him he heard Lyle enter the attic.

Annoyed, Mr. Primm glanced back. "Just checking the boiler," he said. *Was he really talking to a crocodile?*

Lyle pulled out something from behind his back. Mr. Primm was surprised to recognize the frame containing his old college wrestling singlet and whistle. What was the crocodile doing with that?

Lyle lifted a claw. It hovered for a moment over the glass front of the frame. Mr. Primm's eyes widened. But before he could protest . . .

CRASH!

With one firm tap, the glass shattered. Lyle carefully swept the broken glass into a corner, then pulled the singlet out of the frame and tossed it to Mr. Primm. Mr. Primm started to catch on to what might be happening here. Slipping quickly into the singlet—it still fit!—he smiled at his reflection in the mirror. Then he licked his fingers eagerly and turned to Lyle, who raised the whistle to his snout. A shrill tone reverberated through the attic.

Lyle rushed forward, slamming Mr. Primm to the ground!

Mr. Primm lay there, winded. Lyle stared worriedly down at the man on the floor in front of him. Had he hit him too hard? He gave Mr. Primm a deeply apologetic look, then sadly turned away, worried that he'd just made things worse instead of better. He wandered back across the attic and headed for the stairs.

The next moment footsteps rang out behind him. Lyle turned to see Mr. Primm standing in the middle of the attic floor, his body again arranged into a wrestling stance!

"Aaaah!" Mr. Primm cried, rushing the crocodile. It had been a while, but his old moves were already coming back to him.

SLAM!

He pinned his huge opponent to the floor.

Now it was Lyle's turn to feel winded. And delighted! He beamed up at Mr. Primm. His plan had worked!

Mr. Primm stared down at him with an expression of utter disbelief. *Did I really just pin a* crocodile *of all things?* he thought, his disbelief rapidly changing to triumph. *Why yes, I believe I* did *just pin a crocodile! Wa-hoo!!*

No sooner had the thought formed in his mind when Lyle bucked, sending him sideways. Mr. Primm bounced off the wall and staggered to his feet. Then, with a roar, he hurled himself back at Lyle.

The wrestling match was short but intense. Mr. Primm and Lyle traded blows and holds and even some WWE moves. It was loud. It was kind of painful. But Mr. Primm loved every moment of it!

Finally he managed to pin Lyle again. "I've still got it! All-State Champs, ninety nine!" he panted.

Lyle just smiled. Anyone watching might have guessed that it would be easy enough for him to flip the man off again and break the pin. But he stayed still, letting Mr. Primm win.

★

Downstairs the mood was less festive. While the whole house shook beneath the force of the wrestling match, Hector managed to convince a nervous Josh and his mother that nothing was wrong. Unfortunately no one thought to venture downstairs to reassure Mr. Grumps, who even more unfortunately happened to be sitting on his toilet when the melee began. The ceiling rocked, the windows rattled, and for a moment Mr. Grumps wondered if there was an earthquake.

But no—he soon realized the problem, as usual, was coming from directly upstairs. Again! He gnashed his teeth as the room swayed. Suddenly the medicine cabinet fell from the wall, shattering all over the floor.

Mr. Grumps just sat there for a moment, boiling fury in his eyes. If he had been a cartoon character, steam would have been coming out of his ears.

But this wasn't a cartoon, and Mr. Grumps was a real-life man who'd finally reached the end of his rope. First his cat, then his sleep, now his apartment—those interlopers upstairs were destroying his peace, his tranquil home, and everything else he cherished!

This had gone on long enough. The time had come for him to put a stop to it.

Once and for all.

Monday morning before homeroom, Mr. Primm's classroom was in its usual state of chaotic cacophony. Girls lounged around, chatting and laughing. A few phones emitted noisy beeps and blasts of sound as their owners played video games, while others rang out with music from the latest Sweep videos.

Suddenly the door slammed open. Mr. Primm stalked in, but nobody paid a bit of attention. As usual.

But today was not going to be an *as usual* kind of day. For one thing, Mr. Primm looked quite different. And not just because of the cut on his lip or the bruises on his face. No, it was his eyes. They were burning with something that hadn't been there in a long time.

Some would call it confidence. Others might call it barely suppressed joie de vivre.

Mr. Primm? He called it *mojo*.

"Good morning, girls," he said.

No response. Mr. Primm had expected that. And he was ready.

He raised the whistle strung around his neck and blew. The ear-shattering result silenced the students instantly. They all turned to stare at their teacher.

"Right." Mr. Primm smiled, knowing he had them. "Let's try this again, shall we?"

★

That afternoon, Josh returned home from school to find Hector rearranging the living room. He announced that he was going to thank the Primms for their hospitality by putting on a show. While Lyle went to make popcorn, Josh and his mother sat down, ready to be entertained.

Hector was busy doing tricks, telling jokes, and treating them to other highlights from his well-practiced act when Mr. Primm came in. Josh waved to him.

"Dad, you've gotta see this!" he exclaimed.

BOOM!

There was an explosion of theatrical smoke. Hector leaped through it, presenting silk flowers, which rapidly changed into fluttering doves, then spinning playing cards that flew through the air like boomerangs.

As the Primms watched, all three of them open-mouthed with astonishment, Hector stepped over to the piano. His fingers flew over the keys, expertly picking out a rollicking tune, as he began to sing.

Lyle emerged from the kitchen with popcorn in a red-and-white–striped bucket. Lyle dumped salt on his snack, and then into his mouth for good measure. A coughing fit briefly distracted him from Hector's song, but then he cocked his head, immediately recognizing the tune. It was the same one he and Hector used to perform. And boy, was Hector performing it now!

Lyle's toe started to tap. He still remembered the words as if he'd sung them only yesterday, rather than a year and a half ago. He couldn't resist joining in quietly, his voice lost beneath Hector's enthusiastic tenor. But on his favorite line, the crocodile's voice rang out fully, echoing through the room.

Hector spun around. So did Josh and his parents.

There was a moment of silence. Everyone stared at Lyle.

Then the crocodile stepped forward to stand beside Hector. Hector grinned and continued the song, and this time Lyle joined in. They sang, and then they started to dance together. The old moves came back quickly, the pair moving in perfect rhythm, finishing the song with a final flourish.

There was another moment of silence. Then the Primms broke into wild applause.

★

Later that night, Hector and Lyle talked in the

attic. Hector's head was full of plans abandoned, ambitions denied, and dreams he'd done his best to banish from his mind long ago—eighteen months ago, to be precise. Now all of his hopes and dreams were back, bigger, bolder, and more exciting than ever.

"Don't you see what this means?" he asked his old friend. "You performed in front of an audience, Lyle!"

Hector jumped to his feet and started pacing. For so long, he'd repressed those old dreams of superstardom. Now, with just one song, they'd come roaring back. He wasn't sure what had happened, or why Lyle was able to sing in front of people other than him. Maybe it was just maturity. Lyle had been awfully young back then, but . . .

"We can do it now!" he exclaimed. "We can actually take our show on the road—you and me, just the way we always planned!"

Lyle gazed back at him, looking deeply uncertain. Hector scarcely noticed. He was so overcome with the possibilities now rushing and tumbling through his mind that he burst out singing again.

Lyle just sat there, feeling anxious and unsettled. Was Hector right? Had he overcome his stage fright at long last? He hoped so, if only because he could tell the idea pleased Hector—and Lyle would do anything he could to please Hector. That was how it had always been.

But he wasn't sure what to think about Hector's plans to take their show on the road. Wouldn't that mean leaving Josh and his parents? Lyle didn't like the thought of that. Not at all. But he also didn't want to let Hector down—again. What would he do if he had to choose between his oldest friend and his new ones? He had no idea, and besides that, the infectious surge of Hector's singing was awfully distracting. Lyle swayed, losing himself in the intoxicating rhythm. After all, maybe Hector was right. Maybe things *could* work out this time. . . .

★

Over the next few days, Hector and Lyle worked hard rehearsing and polishing up their act. Hector was feeling good about the future. Lyle's singing sounded great—better than ever, actually. Now that the crocodile had overcome his stage fright, nothing could stop them!

Naturally, though, Hector would have to prove that they were ready. That was how show business worked. He would start by staging a preview for some investors. Hector and Lyle would wow them into financing the world tour Hector was already busy planning.

Between rehearsals Hector worked the phone, talking his way into an open spot at a local theater. Once they nailed the preview, which was only a formality, the world would be their oyster! Hector was already imagining his name (and Lyle's, too, of course, though perhaps in slightly smaller letters) spelled out in neon lights in front of every major theater from Broadway to London to Tokyo. He couldn't wait!

When the big night arrived, Hector descended from the attic with Lyle in tow. Hector was practically buzzing with energy and barely noticed

Josh noticing them leaving. "Where are you going?" Josh asked as Hector swept by.

"The preview! For potential investors in our new show," Hector said, with barely a backward glance.

Josh considered Lyle. "But does he want that?" he asked, observing that his friend did not, Josh thought, seem to want that.

"He's a performer, Josh!" Hector replied. And it seemed there would be no more discussion on the matter.

Josh followed Hector and Lyle out the back door of the brownstone. "Evangelyne will get us there in time," Hector told them.

"Who's Evangelyne?" Josh asked.

Instead of answering, Hector grabbed the handle of a filthy garage door covered with graffiti that Josh had never even noticed before. He slammed it open, then disappeared into the gloom.

"Hector?" Josh called.

There was an explosion of noise somewhere inside, echoing into the street. A moment later Hector reappeared, this time driving an ancient-looking motorbike with a matching sidecar. He tossed Lyle a helmet. Lyle pulled it on and squeezed himself into the sidecar.

Hector twisted the throttle, and Evangelyne responded with a throaty roar. Lyle looked at Josh. A look that said "I wish you could come" and "I'm sorry." Hector, again, didn't notice. He gave Josh a sloppy salute before gunning the engine and disappearing into the night.

I t was late by the time Hector and Lyle returned to the house on East 88th Street, though all three Primms were still awake. They couldn't bear to go to bed before hearing what had happened at the investor preview show.

Hector came in first, his expressive face a roiling storm of dark emotions. Josh leaped to his feet.

"How'd it go?" he asked eagerly.

Hector didn't respond. He just headed for the stairs.

"Hector?" Josh said.

Hector kept walking. "Show biz can be a cruel mistress," he muttered over his shoulder.

Josh followed him up the stairs. "What does that mean?"

"I thought things had changed," Hector said

with a sigh. "I thought *Lyle* had changed . . ."

His voice trailed off, and he glanced toward the back door. Lyle had just come in looking crestfallen.

". . . but he hasn't," Hector finished grimly. "He still won't sing."

With a final shake of his head, Hector disappeared up the attic steps.

Josh shot a worried look at Lyle, who hung his head. Even his tail looked limp and sad. Josh went to him, stretching his arms to draw the huge crocodile into a comforting hug.

"Just so you know," Josh told him, "I don't care whether you sing or not. I think you're awesome either way."

Crocodile tears have an unfortunate reputation. But the ones welling up in Lyle's eyes at that moment were unquestionably sincere.

Josh watched his friend make his way upstairs, quietly singing the last few bars of his and Hector's signature song. It was normally an up-tempo foot-tapper of a tune, but right then it sounded more like a dirge.

★

In the attic, Hector was hurriedly stripping off his tuxedo. Lyle watched sadly.

"I won't pretend this isn't something of a blow, old friend," Hector told him. "One or two outstanding loans will now require some, er, radical renegotiation." He tossed Lyle a brave smile. "But it's nothing I can't smooth over with a little Valenti charm!"

With that, he flung open the attic window. Lyle sighed and hung his head in shame. He'd done it again—he'd let Hector down.

★

The next day, Mr. Primm was walking home after work when he noticed a commotion outside Mr. Grumps's apartment. Carol, the woman from the school, was there, and seemed to be arguing with Mr. Grumps. Meanwhile various other people were filing into the apartment. Mr. Primm vaguely recognized some of them—neighbors from up and down the block.

In a frustrated tone Mr. Primm could hear

from where he stood, Carol told Mr. Grumps "There really is nothing more to say." Then she turned and stomped away, glowering. When she reached Mr. Primm, she shoved a crumpled document into his hands. "Mr. Primm," she said curtly. "For you."

She took off before Mr. Primm was able to respond. As he started to uncrumple the papers she'd given him, Mr. Grumps came toward him with a smirk on his face.

"Oh, good," Mr. Grumps said. "It's the man of the hour! You're a member of the neighborhood, right? Well, it's time to earn your spot."

"Okay," Mr. Primm said tentatively. "Great."

Mr. Grumps disappeared back inside. Before Mr. Primm could even begin to figure out what was going on, he heard the squeal of tires turning onto the block far too fast. The car slowed slightly in front of the brownstone. The back door flew open, and a figure burst out, tumbling over and over on the sidewalk before somehow landing on his feet in a *ta-da* pose that would have done any gymnast proud. Mr. Primm could clearly hear someone inside the car scream "Get the money!" before the engine revved and they sped away.

Hector grabbed his hat from the pavement, where it had landed during his tumble. Noticing Mr. Primm at last, he simply said "show business," as if that explained anything at all. As rapidly as he could manage, Hector limped up the steps toward the brownstone's front door, while Mr. Primm looked on in astonishment.

Mr. Primm glanced from Hector to Mr. Grumps's line of visitors and back again. He had the uneasy feeling that the two might just be connected somehow. There was only one way to find out. . . .

When he entered Mr. Grumps's fastidiously tidy living room, he was surprised to see his wife already sitting there. He took a seat beside her, glancing around at the other occupants. With a sinking heart, he realized what this was: a meeting of the local Neighborhood Association, the very same organization that Mr. Grumps had been threatening them with from the moment they'd arrived.

Mr. Grumps stood in front of the group. His

eyes glittered with something that might have been malice as he glanced at the Primms.

"I don't want to be unneighborly," he began, his voice nearly as gentle and sweet as his eyes were cold and focused. "Really I don't. Maybe wanting a little peace and quiet just seems, well, unreasonable. Old-fashioned."

"No, no," one of the neighbors said reassuringly.

"What do you mean?" another added.

A third shook her head. "Absolutely not!"

Mr. Grumps glanced again at the Primms, holding both hands to his heart. "We all just want to live happily together in this community." He turned to the others. "Because that's exactly what we are, aren't we?" Noticing that the cup in front of a crabby-looking old woman was getting low, he grabbed a carafe. "Marjory, a little more decaf?"

He carefully filled her cup. Then he set down the carafe and continued.

"And the point is, no one loves music and singing and dancing more than me." He paused for effect, glancing around the room to make sure all attention was on him. "Just not at three o'clock in the morning."

The other neighbors let out a sigh of agreement. Marjory nodded vigorously.

"So please," Mr. Grumps continued, "find it in your hearts to sign this petition and override the school's power to allow awful families to reside among us."

He stared at the Primms on the last line, barely concealing a triumphant smirk. Mr. Primm lifted his hand.

"Please," he began, "could we just have a chance to . . ."

THUMP!

Everyone looked up at the ceiling. Then all eyes turned to the Primms. Some of the eyes were hostile. Many were merely disapproving.

"Josh has, uh . . ." Mr. Primm cast his mind around for an excuse, something that might explain the thumping coming from upstairs.

"A trampoline!" his wife jumped in helpfully.

"Wrestling practice," Mr. Primm finished at the same time.

"Josh wrestling on the trampoline that we are going to get rid of," Mrs. Primm plowed on. "It's no problem!"

Mr. Grumps's lips quirked upward in the tiniest of smiles. He had them on the ropes now, and he knew it. He pulled out his petition and a handful of pens, passing them around.

"And if you're hiding something in that apartment," he told the Primms icily, "something you think you're going to get in trouble for, I believe now would be the time to share it."

The eyes of the other neighbors swiveled once more toward the Primms. Now most of them looked curious. What could Mr. Grumps be referring to?

"Do you mind if I join you?"

Everyone's eyes swiveled yet again. Mr. Primm's heart sank. Hector sashayed into the room, his voice and expression as cocky as ever, even though his clothes were dirty and torn, his nose trickled blood, and a black-and-blue humdinger of a shiner was rapidly forming over one eye.

"Valenti?" Mr. Grumps exclaimed, his jaw dropping.

Hector peered at him. "As I live and breathe!" he exclaimed. *"Alistair Grumps!* How in the devil are you?" He slung an arm around the other man's shoulders. "Is that the same sofa? You literally *have not* changed a thing, have you?" He grinned around at the rest of the room. "You see, Alistair and I grew up together."

Mr. Grumps pulled away, scowling. Hector barely seemed to notice. He was beaming at Mr. Grumps with nostalgic delight.

"Get out," Mr. Grumps spat at him. "This is none of your business."

"But if the Primms are the problem, then as their houseguest I'm part of the problem, too, am I not?" Hector pointed out with impeccable logic.

Mr. Grumps frowned. "A very large part."

"Then with your permission I would very much like to be part of the solution." Hector settled himself on the sofa between Mr. and Mrs. Primm. He threw his arms around them.

"Per usual, Hector," Mr. Grumps said through a clenched jaw, "you're overstepping."

"But we aren't the only ones who overstep the mark, are we?" Suddenly Hector's eyes went just as sharp and focused as Mr. Grumps's own. "We, for instance, haven't mounted security cameras throughout the neighborhood—have we?"

Mr. Grumps froze. Everyone turned to stare at him. But Hector wasn't finished.

"*Filming* other residents," he went on, enunciating each word carefully, "*without* their consent . . ."

Now even the Primms were staring at Mr. Grumps. He gulped. Was it hot in here?

"Was permission asked?" Hector wondered aloud. "Were releases signed? If it was me, I'd go straight to the police."

Mr. Grumps looked decidedly uncomfortable now. It was time to end this ghastly moment. "Out!" he shouted. "All of you!"

The Neighborhood Association members allowed him to herd them toward the door. The Primms went, too, relieved to have the meeting end.

"Everyone out!" Mr. Grumps ordered, pushing one man, waving his hands to hurry an older woman along. "This meeting will reconvene at a later date." Seeing Hector wandering out after the rest, he glowered at him. "Not you," he hissed.

Hector looked back at his old acquaintance. "I can assure you, Alistair, we have absolutely nothing else to talk about."

Mr. Grumps narrowed his eyes. "Why don't we see about that."

The Primms were waiting for Hector in the living room when he walked in a short while later. "Thank you, Hector," Mrs. Primm greeted him, dabbing at the scratches on his face with a handkerchief. "Thank you so much."

"You were extraordinary," Mr. Primm added.

Josh glanced over from the sofa, where he and Lyle were playing video games. He wasn't sure what was going on. All he knew was that his parents had come in babbling about the cranky downstairs neighbor.

"On the contrary," Hector said, sounding rather weary. "You have all been extraordinary, and it was the least I could do." He gazed at them for a moment. "Now if you'll excuse me, I should make myself presentable." He swept into a bow.

"Back in two shakes of a lamb's tail."

At that, Lyle abruptly twisted around and stared at Hector, watching wide-eyed as the man disappeared up the stairs.

A few minutes later the mournful wail of an emergency siren wound its way down the block. Mrs. Primm stepped to the window and looked out just as a police car screeched to a halt at the curb. Right behind it was a van with big letters on the side: ANIMAL CONTROL UNIT.

"Hide him!" Mrs. Primm gasped.

When Josh saw the van, he grabbed Lyle. "Stay here!" he ordered frantically, shoving the crocodile into a closet.

He slammed the door and raced upstairs. Hector was the only one who might be able to fix this!

But when he burst into the attic, his jaw dropped in shock. It was empty. All of Hector's belongings were gone—the clothes, the stage makeup, the props, even the cot. The window was wide open, curtains flapping in the breeze.

By the time Josh got downstairs again, everything was in chaos. The house was filled with uniformed police talking grimly into their two-way radios, animal control officers barking orders at one another while wielding nets, and his parents shouting and waving their arms in dismay. Lyle's hiding place had been discovered, and now he huddled in the middle of the room, looking terrified.

"No!" Josh yelled as he spotted one of the officers raising a tranquilizer gun.

He jumped in front of Lyle, flinging his arms wide to protect his friend. The officer froze, finger quivering over the trigger.

"He won't hurt you!" Josh cried.

But another officer grabbed Josh, yanking him out of the way. Josh struggled and shouted, but it was no use—the adults were too strong for him.

★

Lyle had been frozen in place, not certain what was happening or what he should do. But seeing the officers manhandling his friend broke him out of his panicked daze. Fear was suddenly replaced by anger. Desperate to protect Josh and desperate to send these people away, Lyle reared up. Then he did the one thing he could think of that sent people running. He roared.

The animal control officers jumped back, terror flashing in their eyes. The officer with the rifle raised it again. . . .

"No!" Josh cried. "Lyle— you have to sing!"

Lyle froze again. That feeling returned—the same one that had grabbed him onstage at the Coney Island Coronet all those months ago. The same feeling that had refused to allow a single note to pass through his throat at the investors' preview show just yesterday.

Singing was Lyle's favorite thing in the world. But not in front of strangers. That was the one thing he couldn't do.

Not even to save himself.

He stared at his young friend, wishing he could explain. Hoping Josh would understand.

PING!

The dart flew out of the rifle and buried

itself in Lyle's side. He barely felt the sting as he crumpled to the ground, and the last sight he saw before his eyes fluttered shut was Josh staring helplessly down at him.

★

Moments later Josh stood with his parents, watching as the doors slammed shut on the animal control van. Lyle was inside. It had taken all the officers' strength to drag the unconscious Lyle out of the house and into the vehicle, but they'd done it. Now they were taking him away, and there was nothing Josh could do to save his friend.

The van peeled out, accompanied by the police car, its lights flashing. Josh stared after them until the vehicles disappeared around the corner. When he glanced up at his parents, they looked almost as devastated as he felt.

Then he noticed something. In the struggle to load Lyle into the van, his old silk scarf must have come loose. It was lying bedraggled on the sidewalk. Josh picked it up and clutched it to his chest.

Just then Mr. Grumps rushed over, his beady eyes sparkling with glee. "I *knew* it!" he exclaimed. "I knew you were up to no good! And thanks to me, everyone else knows it now, too." He glared at the Primms. "A *crocodile*, hidden in your brownstone? You've broken so many rules, told so many lies, you're in more trouble than anyone I've ever met. Forget this *building*, wait until I tell your school!" He jabbed a righteous finger at Mr. Primm. "You'll be unemployable. They'll throw you out of the *city*, they'll throw you out of the *state!*" His lip curled with triumph. "You'll be gone, all of you, by Thanksgiving!"

With that, he spun on his heel and marched triumphantly back to his apartment, disappearing inside.

The Primms stood there, not speaking. What, after all, was there to say? Lyle was gone.

A zoo can be a pleasant place for a person to while away an afternoon. It can even be an acceptable residence for an animal who was born in captivity and knows nothing else.

But for a crocodile accustomed to the finer things in life, such as friends, bubble baths, imported caviar, and—most of all—freedom, it can feel like a prison cell. And that was precisely how it felt to Lyle.

He lay sadly on the edge of a wide pool surrounded by large rocks. Several other crocodiles were nearby, staring at him with a combination of curiosity and hostility. After a moment they moved as a group—or rather, a *bask*, as a group of crocodiles is properly called—turning their scaly backs to the newcomer.

Well, all except for the oldest croc in the pen.

He farted loudly. *Then* he turned his back.

Lyle sighed. His eyes drifted half shut. . . .

"Lyle!"

The familiar voice startled him out of his stupor. He sat up, heart beating with new hope, and saw Josh running toward the crocodile enclosure. Mr. and Mrs. Primm were right behind him.

Lyle rushed to meet his friend. A line of six-foot-tall iron bars separated them. Lyle held his clawed hand up just the same. Quietly, each of the Primms extended a finger, touching Lyle's smooth scales, trying to get as close to him as the bars would allow.

It was Josh who broke the silence. "We have to *do* something," he cried. "He must *hate* it here!"

Behind Lyle, a door opened and a zookeeper entered the pen. The keeper was carrying a couple of large buckets filled with fish. She tipped them out and noticed the Primms. "Keep your hands away from the bars!" she yelled as the other crocodiles slid across the rocks and eagerly started gulping down the fish.

"They understand crocodiles here, Josh," Mr.

Primm said uncertainly, watching the bask feed. "They'll look after him."

Josh only clutched the bars tighter. "Then why aren't they giving him pork and rosemary vol-au-vents?" he demanded. "Or chicken Milanese with a dash of salsa verde and some pomme puree?"

"He's a crocodile," Mrs. Primm reminded her son. "We know he's a very unusual crocodile—but he's still a crocodile. He has to learn to live with other crocodiles now."

Josh glanced around and lowered his voice. "We can break him out!" he whispered.

"Darling—" his mother began.

"It's not a bank," Josh went on, "it's a zoo! How hard can it be?"

Mr. Primm shook his head. "Josh, stop. We'll visit Lyle every day."

"Yes," Mrs. Primm agreed. "And we'll speak to the zoo and see if they'll let us bring some of his favorite snacks."

"But there's only so much we can do," Mr. Primm added. "Not all problems have a solution, Josh."

Josh frowned at his parents. "You don't get to decide that!" he cried. "Not for me, not anymore! All my life I've been scared, because *you've* been scared." He met Lyle's eye. "But I'm not scared anymore—because of Lyle. He changed everything. You know he did. Not just for me, but for *you*, too!" He turned back to his parents and squared his shoulders. "And I don't care what you say," he told them firmly. "I am *not* leaving here without . . . without . . ." He let out a wheeze, then blinked rapidly several times.

"Josh?" Mrs. Primm exclaimed as Lyle sat straight up in alarm.

Josh had just crumpled to the ground!

★

Josh woke up in the back of an FDNY ambulance. When he glanced out the rear doors, he saw they were parked just outside the zoo gates. Paramedics hustled around, checking him over.

"He had a panic attack that triggered his asthma," one of the paramedics told Mr. and Mrs. Primm. "It was serious, but it's good that he had his inhaler with him." The paramedic gave the parents a supportive smile. "You did everything right, and he's going to be fine. You've got nothing to worry about."

Mr. Primm was still staring at Josh. "You all right, buddy?" he asked, his eyes searching Josh's downturned face.

"Yeah," Josh said quietly.

"You sure?" Mr. Primm put his arm around his son. Josh was too sad to do more than nod in reply.

Mr. and Mrs. Primm looked relieved as they thanked everyone for coming to the rescue. But Josh knew that the paramedic was wrong. He did have something to worry about—Lyle. How was his friend ever going to survive without his family?

★

Later that night, Lyle found himself wondering the same thing. While the other crocodiles slept, he began singing softly.

It was a mournful tune, soaring and sad, that brought to mind all the memories he'd shared with the Primms. Thinking back over the time since they'd come to East 88th Street—and into his life—made Lyle feel happy, but somehow sad at the same time. This was even worse than when Hector had left him alone in that attic. Because at least then he'd still had hope.

It was a difficult night for everyone. At the house on East 88th Street, Josh curled up on the attic floor, Lyle's scarf in his hands. He slept fitfully, dreaming of those thrilling nights out with Lyle, leaping and climbing over the rooftops of the city. Would he ever feel that happy and free again?

Mrs. Primm walked heavily up the stairs, glancing wistfully at one of the portraits she'd painted of Lyle. The dark, quiet house was full of memories of their afternoons together, making a joyful mess of paints or powdered sugar— memories of being with Lyle, having the time of her life.

In the bedroom, Mr. Primm opened a drawer and looked at his carefully folded wrestling singlet. His old whistle lay on top of it, and he could still hear the shrill and thrilling sound it made when Lyle blew it. He guessed they'd never wrestle together again.

Near the back of a Greyhound bus lumbering out of the city, Hector P. Valenti sat slumped in his seat. He counted the cash Mr. Grumps had given him and wondered gloomily if he'd underestimated how much to charge when selling his soul.

Then there was Mr. Grumps himself. Unlike the others, he wasn't feeling the least bit sad. His feelings were all happiness and glee. He'd *won*!

But when he called Loretta for dinner, the cat turned up her delicate nose for the first time ever. She stalked away to the other end of the apartment—aloof and regal, with every silky hair on her body saying quite clearly that she preferred to be alone.

Back at the zoo, the last notes of Lyle's song rose into the clear night sky. The other crocodiles were awake now, floating in their pool and watching their strange new companion pour his heart out. But most crocodiles don't have much use for music or singing, however heartfelt it might be. In unison, they all sank beneath the water.

Leaving Lyle completely and utterly alone.

At school the next day, Josh sat by himself in the cafeteria staring at his food. He had no appetite. All he could think about was poor Lyle, stuck in that cage.

Trudy rushed over to his table. "Can you believe it?" she cried, sounding excited. "I still can't believe it! My dance crew is actually going to be on *Show Us What You Got!*" She did a little dance step right then and there, unable to stand still.

Josh was happy for her. At least as happy as he could possibly be, given that he was completely and utterly miserable.

"That's . . . great," he managed to mumble. He tried to smile to make his words sound more sincere, but it didn't quite work. "You deserve it," he added sadly.

Trudy gazed down at him. Everyone in school

had heard about what had happened to Josh's pet crocodile, and she was pretty sure she knew how he was feeling. Namely, bad. Wanting to make him feel better, she sat down and gave him a sympathetic look.

"Don't give up, that's all I'm saying," she advised. "When Malfoy escaped I thought I was never going to see him again either."

Josh stared at her blankly.

"Malfoy," Trudy prompted. "The pet rattlesnake my uncle Ernie gave me." She shrugged. "Malfoy was gone for six weeks—we all thought he was dead."

Josh sighed. Okay, so at least Lyle wasn't dead. Was that Trudy's point? If so, it wasn't making him feel much better.

But Trudy wasn't finished. "Then one day the neighbors found him," she said. "He was curled up in the back of their toaster oven." She smiled, picked up the cookie from her tray, broke it in half, and handed it to him. "Miracles do happen, Josh."

Josh took the cookie from Trudy and mustered

a small, sad smile. "There he goes," his friend said with an encouraging smile in return.

★

Mrs. Primm was waiting for Josh outside school that afternoon. He wasn't exactly surprised to see her there. "I'm fine," he assured her, by way of greeting.

"I know you're fine," she said, not at all sure that either of them were.

That evening, the Primms sat silently around the dining table. There was no music. No laughter. Just the occasional scrape of a fork against a plate.

Josh kept glancing at the empty seat beside him. Lyle's seat. He'd set it with a plate, glass, and silverware before remembering. After that, he hadn't had the heart to put the stuff away.

BANG!

It was just an ordinary street noise, probably a truck backfiring or something. The type of sound that happened all over the busy city all the time. But this time, it made the whole family jump.

Josh stood up. "I'll take the trash out," he said.

"Okay," said Mrs. Primm.

"Be careful," Mr. Primm added.

Josh gave them a long look. He knew his parents were worried after seeing him pass out at the zoo. They'd barely let him out of their sight since the incident had happened. He had to get away for a second, just to be alone and think in peace.

He grabbed the bag of trash and headed out the back door. As he walked across the courtyard to the trash cans, he stopped short when a figure materialized out of the darkness. For a second he felt nervous.

Hector P. Valenti stepped forward. He didn't look quite like himself. Oh, he was still dressed in his cape and odd clothes, that part was the same. It was more about the man *inside* the clothes. Somehow, that man looked smaller than usual. Less confident. Wary of the world. He barely dared to meet Josh's eye.

Josh tossed the bag into a trash can and closed the lid with a slam. "How could you do it?" he demanded, his mind suddenly filled with images of Lyle lying in that pen at the zoo, completely miserable. He'd spent a while blaming Mr. Grumps for what had happened. But then he'd realized there was no way the neighbor could have known about Lyle unless someone had told him. Someone like Hector P. Valenti, who *just happened* to have vanished without a trace right when the animal control officers arrived.

"I've asked myself that same question over and over," Hector replied. "I've got nothing, Josh. No family, no friends. All I ever had was Lyle."

Josh frowned. "They why do you keep *leaving him*?"

That silenced Hector. When he didn't respond, Josh turned and continued toward the trash cans.

"You want the truth?" Hector called after him.

Josh stopped short. He was waiting.

"When Lyle choked, I had to go back out and make it on my own." Hector shook his head. "But I couldn't. Because no one's interested in a show with just . . . me. And I owe a lot of people a lot of money, Josh." He stared at the boy, who had turned to look at him. "So when Grumps offered me that cash, I took it—out of weakness, out of fear. And I've hated myself ever since."

"Good," Josh said. "Because I hate you, too."

Hector took a half step toward him. "But this isn't about me anymore," he said, his voice suddenly urgent, his eyes beginning to flash with their usual verve. "It's about Lyle. And you know as well as I do that we can't just leave him in that zoo."

Josh didn't say anything. But he didn't turn away. He listened as Hector went on.

"So if you have the stomach for it," Hector said, now sounding a lot more like his old self, "if you have the kind of fire in your belly I think you have, well then, you, young man, are going to help me *break that crocodile out of the zoo!*"

For a moment Josh just stared at him. He'd trusted Hector before and ended up disappointed. But if he really had a plan to rescue Lyle . . .

"We have *magic* on our side, Josh!" Reaching out, he whipped a coin out from behind Josh's ear. "The *power of illusion!*" With a wave of his hand, the coin disappeared. "The willing suspension of *disbelief*!"

Josh shook his head. He should have known. Hector didn't have a plan. And doing a few silly tricks wasn't going to suddenly turn him into someone Josh—or Lyle—could count on.

"There is no magic, Hector." He grabbed Hector's other hand and turned it over, revealing the coin hidden there. Then he pushed past him toward the door.

"Tonight, Josh!" Hector called after him. "I'll be at the East Sixty-Third Street entrance at eight p.m. sharp! Be there!"

The only response from Josh was the slam of the brownstone's back door.

By day, the venerable swath of nature that lies right down the middle of the isle of Manhattan—the 843 acres better known as Central Park—is a green oasis. It's a place for city dwellers to escape the concrete jungle for rolling lawns, tall trees, and big sky. But it's after darkness falls that the park seems much more like the world's truly wild places—murky, shadowy, and faintly mysterious.

At the very edge of the park, just off East 63rd Street, a figure nearly as mysterious as the place itself swept into view, swirling its cape theatrically.

It was Hector, of course.

He pulled out a pocket watch. The crystal face reflected the glow of the streetlights, revealing that Hector was in full stage makeup. His shoulders sunk slightly as he realized it was well past eight p.m.

Josh wasn't coming. Hector was in this alone.

He stood there a moment longer. Then he squared his shoulders, swept his cape around again, and exited stage right.

At the same time, a zoo security guard was at his desk, feet up and TV on. The job of nighttime security guard wasn't particularly taxing most of the time. Occasionally he had to chase off kids trying to sneak into the zoo after hours. Once, images flickering on the surveillance screens beside his TV had caught a mugging just outside the zoo's perimeter. The guard had called the NYPD. He'd been treated as a hero for about five minutes after that, which had been kind of cool. Otherwise? His job consisted mostly of a lot of TV reruns and boredom.

He watched with mild interest as an ad popped onscreen for that night's live finale of *Show Us What You Got!*, which was due to air in less than an hour. Suddenly a flicker of movement from one of the security screens caught his eye. He frowned and leaned forward. Then, with a sigh, he heaved himself to his feet and headed outside.

By the time the guard reached the main entrance gate, the odd-looking figure he'd spotted hadn't moved on as he'd hoped. In fact, he was peering into the zoo with both hands clutching the bars of the gate.

"My dear fellow," the man called. "I wonder if I may request some assistance."

The guard frowned, giving the stranger a once-over. Was he actually wearing a *cape*?

Then he noticed something else. The man's hands were handcuffed to the bars!

Hector shot the man a sheepish smile. "I thought I had this trick down," he said. "But I appear to have got myself in a bit of a pickle."

This wasn't the first colorful character the guard had encountered, for in addition to muggers and mischievous kids, the park at night was the domain of some unusual people who stayed hidden in daylight hours but found freedom after dark.

The guard stepped forward, already imagining

how he'd tell this story to the guy who took over at the end of his shift. As he leaned down to examine the cuffs, there was a sudden flurry of movement on the other side of the gate.

"Magical Magic!" Hector cried.

Now it was the guard who found himself handcuffed to the gate! He shouted with dismay, but Hector was already reaching through the bars and nimbly lifting the keys from the man's belt. Seconds later, he was inside.

"I promise you this won't take long," he reassured the guard as he swept past, following signs pointing the way to the Reptile Pavilion.

★

Hector's heart beat fast with excitement. He removed a long, long, loooong line of knotted rope made from his collection of silk handkerchiefs from his pocket and lowered it over the wall of the crocodile enclosure. He'd pulled off a lot of fabulous moments of stagecraft over the years, along with a few shady offstage exploits, but this was shaping up to be Hector's most thrilling heist yet.

He clambered down the rope and jumped off at the bottom. It was dark in this part of the pen, away from the security lights. There was one puddle of dim light coming through a large, glass underground viewing window where visitors could observe the crocodiles up close. Hector stood there peering into the gloom beyond.

"Lyle!" he stage-whispered.

There was no response. He edged forward, willing his eyes to adjust to the shadowy dimness.

"Lyle!" A little louder.

This time he caught a flash of movement out of the corner of his eye. He turned and saw a huge crocodile crawling into the patch of light. It snarled.

Hector froze. "*Not* Lyle," he whispered.

He moved backward, reaching for his rope. But when he grabbed it, a knot unraveled and the whole thing fell into the pen!

"*Not* good," Hector said with a gulp.

He stared at the advancing crocodile. The crocodile stared back, its reptilian eyes cold, calculating . . . and hungry.

A sudden noise behind him made Hector spin around, fearing that another toothy predator was sneaking up on him. Instead he saw a small, pale face peering at him from the other side of the viewing window.

"This was seriously your plan?" Josh said, his voice slightly muffled by the glass.

Despite his currently precarious situation, Hector broke into a grin. "I *knew* you'd come!" he cried.

At that moment another crocodile slithered into view nearby. Hector gulped.

"Josh," he said urgently. "Climb up there and catch my rope when I toss it to you. You have to get me out of here!"

He took a step toward the spot where the rope had fallen. But only one step. Because as soon as he moved, several more crocodiles materialized, encircling him. They snarled, creeping closer.

"Lyle!" Josh called.

Hector's eyes widened as another, much more familiar crocodile appeared out of the gloom. Lyle looked up at Josh and smiled.

But when Lyle looked over at Hector, that smile disappeared. Lyle didn't move as the other crocodiles crept still closer. . . .

"Talk to him, Josh!" Hector cried, frantic, not understanding how Lyle could even think about abandoning him at his time of greatest vulnerability. "Lyle! Help me!" he pleaded, searching for some recognition in his old friend's face.

"It's not me who has to talk to him, Hector," Josh replied. "It's *you*."

Hector stared at Lyle. The chorus of snarls surrounding them was getting louder. And now the crocs were adding a bit of percussion to the melody by way of snapping their jaws. Hector knew he didn't have much time. He had to get this right, or this could be—*would* be—his final curtain call.

"I realize I may have made some mistakes," he blurted out. "And, er, perhaps haven't always acted in the best way possible. But I showed you the world, Lyle! I introduced you to white truffle oil. I taught you to moonwalk!"

Hector risked a quick peek at the other

crocodiles. They loomed all around him, inches away now. But Lyle remained unmoved.

Hector's life flashed before his eyes. That life had had its difficult moments, sure, its ups and downs and in-betweens, but overall it was a pretty fabulous life, and he wasn't ready to give it up.

"Fine, fine, fine!" he cried desperately. "I apologize completely. My behavior was unforgivable. I used you, I abandoned you, and it's my fault you're here."

Behind the glass, Josh looked surprised. Hector's apology was better than he'd expected.

But Hector wasn't finished. He had to make Lyle see that he meant it this time—that he'd never leave him behind again. "Please, Lyle," he pleaded. "You have to come with me. You have to come back to where you belong!"

Still Lyle didn't move. Hector glanced toward Josh for help.

But Josh was watching Lyle. The moment Lyle met Josh's eye and smiled again, Hector finally caught on to what was happening here.

Lyle was no longer his crocodile.

He was Josh's.

"Back to . . . Josh," Hector added. "And the Primms."

Lyle finally turned toward him, a question in his eyes.

But that question came a moment too late. One of the other crocodiles had run out of patience.

Its huge jaws full of razor-sharp teeth wide open, it lunged at Hector.

Josh gasped at the massive crocodile's deadly speed. But Lyle was a crocodile, too, and he was motivated by something even stronger than hunger. Leaping forward, he grabbed the crocodile's tail in his jaws and sent him flying, right past Hector, landing against the bars beyond.

Whew! That had been close.

The other crocodiles stared at Lyle, and if a bask of crocs could look astonished, that was how they looked. But Josh suspected it wouldn't be long before their beady eyes returned to Hector.

Hector seemed to realize it, too. "Right," he said. "Let's get out of here."

He looked at Lyle. But Lyle was looking at Josh again. Josh noticed Hector's crestfallen expression, but was unmoved. Lyle hadn't been Hector's crocodile for a while now. It was about time he realized it.

"Hector's right," Josh told his friend. "We have to get you out of here."

The knotted handkerchief rope was stronger than it looked—strong enough even for the weight of a massive crocodile. Just barely, but just barely was enough.

Soon Josh, Lyle, and Hector were sprinting for the zoo gate. "Tell me the second part of your plan is better than the first," Josh panted as he ran.

"Not just better," Hector assured him, "it's *perfect*. I've got Evangelyne parked up on Sixty-Third. We can outrun anyone on Evangelyne."

"But Lyle can't just keep running," Josh protested.

"Of course he can!" Hector shrugged. "You'd be amazed what you can outrun, Josh. Creditors, law enforcement officials . . ."

The words were barely out of his mouth before several guards appeared. A park security cart came to a halt, blocking the gate.

Josh screeched to a stop. "But that's not a life," he said.

Hector looked confused. Because, as Josh was starting to realize, that was *his* life. Hector P. Valenti had spent most of his days on the run in one way or another, sometimes figuratively, all too often literally. This was the life he'd chosen, so maybe it was okay for him. But it was no kind of life for Lyle.

"We have to show people what Lyle can do," Josh said. "We have to show them, once and for all, that they don't have to be scared of him."

So close, and yet so far, Josh thought, shooting a wistful look toward the street just outside the gate. At that moment a city bus rumbled past. Plastered on its side was an ad for the *Show Us What You Got!* live finale that very night at nine.

Josh looked over at Hector. Hector looked back at Josh. And for once, the two of them understood each other perfectly.

"Go," Hector said. "Take Lyle." He glanced at the guards. "I've got this."

He dramatically threw his arms into the air. A pair of metal hoops appeared in his hands.

"Sorry, not that," he said, tossing them away.

He flung up his hands again. This time a full deck of playing cards waterfalled into view, scattering all over the ground.

"Give me a minute," Hector muttered.

He took a deep breath, obviously doing his best to focus. Josh waited, crossing his fingers.

"Prepare to have your flabber truly gasted!" Hector exclaimed.

Suddenly there was a loud explosion. Purple smoke billowed out of nowhere, obscuring the entire scene. The security guards let out a shout of confusion, there was the sound of running feet . . .

Josh and Lyle didn't stick around to hear any more. This was it! They took off running as fast as a boy and a crocodile could run. As it turned out, a crocodile could run a little faster. But Josh did his best to keep up, following Lyle onto the street and partway down the block. He caught up just as Lyle reached the ancient motorbike hidden in a clump of undergrowth at the edge of the park.

Josh skidded to a stop, staring at Evangelyne. "No," he blurted out.

Lyle looked at him. Josh gulped.

"Lyle, it's a deathtrap!" he protested. "And we've got no one to drive it!"

Lyle climbed into the sidecar, then tossed him a helmet. When Josh caught it, he saw something stuck inside.

His eyes widened. It was his old collector's card—the one he'd given to Lyle soon after they'd met. The plus-four strength card.

Strength. Was that what Lyle was offering him right now?

For a split second, Josh wasn't sure he was up to it. He looked at Evangelyne. Scary.

Then he looked at Lyle.

Not scary. He needed to prove that to everyone.

Jamming the helmet on his head, Josh leaped onto the motorbike and kicked down on the starter.

Nothing happened.

He kicked down again. Still nothing.

Lyle's massive tail snaked up out of the sidecar. Brushing Josh's foot aside, it slammed down on the starter.

VRRROOOOOOOOM!

Evangelyne exploded to life with such force

that Josh nearly tipped over backward. But he held on, tentatively opening the throttle and easing the motorbike out from the bushes toward the busy traffic careening down Fifth Avenue.

★

Back in the zoo security office, Hector was slumped in a chair, handcuffed—with real cuffs, not the trick kind—to a pipe on the wall. A surveillance screen caught Evangelyne as she roared away from the park, with several animal control officers giving chase close behind.

"Come on, Josh!" Hector cried hopefully.

A staticky voice came over the security guard's walkie-talkie. *"They've left the park. Call it in!"*

Yes! Hector had known Josh had it in him. He tried to pump his fist in triumph, but the handcuffs got in the way.

Besides, he had work to do. The security guard was rushing to the other end of the office to grab the phone and call the police. Hector had to act fast to buy Josh and Lyle some time.

"Alakazam!" he cried, shaking his sleeve.

A small marble dropped out onto the floor. Hector frowned at it.

Then he tried again. This time a whole flood of marbles came pouring out of his sleeve, along with some jacks and other random objects. The tiny balls rolled across the floor and under the security guard's foot. He slipped, he slid . . .

CRASH!

He landed hard, his head hitting something on the way down. He lay there unconscious.

Hector gulped. That had been a bit more dramatic than expected.

★

Evangelyne roared down the street, weaving in and out through traffic as if she had a mind of her own. Josh held on for dear life, steering more by instinct than thought. Occasionally he risked a glance at the GPS on his phone, but doing that made him a little seasick, so he tossed the phone to Lyle.

"How much farther?" Josh called over the growl of the engine.

Lyle caught the phone, but his finger accidentally closed the GPS directions and launched a face-replace app instead. He found himself staring at an image of his own face turned into a poodle with its tongue sticking out. Lyle stuck his tongue out, too.

Josh didn't notice. He was too busy trying to hold on as Evangelyne skidded around a corner, leaving the squeal of tires and a puff of black exhaust in her wake.

Then he spotted a huge, brightly colored poster across the front of a theater just ahead. **SHOW US WHAT YOU GOT!** the poster screamed.

Josh hauled on the handlebars, using every ounce of strength he had to turn Evangelyne toward the theater. Luckily the doors were standing wide open.

SCREEEEEEEEEECH!

They slid directly into the lobby, skidding to a halt. A few people screamed at their big entrance. Josh smiled.

"We made it!" he cried.

At that moment on East 88th Street, Mr. Primm was standing in front of the fridge nibbling on a cold slice of pizza. Suddenly his wife ran in, looking frantic.

"Where's Josh?" she cried. "He's not in his room!"

Mr. Primm pulled out his phone and opened the app they used to track Josh's location. His eyes widened and the pizza dropped to the floor, unnoticed.

"What's he doing in Times Square?" he exclaimed.

The Primms stared at each other in horror. Then they bolted for the door.

26

Josh and Lyle found their way backstage by following a series of signs that pointed them down some stairs and along a corridor. They rushed to the end, where they were brought up short by a locked door.

Josh stared at it. Now what?

As if in answer to his question, Trudy pushed open the backstage door. "What are you doing here?" she exclaimed, shocked to find Josh Primm standing there. And he wasn't alone.

Trudy's brown eyes widened as she took in the sight of the crocodile. Its massive body filled the cramped corridor. Even for the coolest, savviest, most confident girl in the entire sixth grade, this was . . . a lot.

"You have to help me, Trudy," Josh begged. "I have to show them what he can do."

Trudy couldn't take her eyes off Lyle. Sure,

she'd known that Josh had a pet crocodile. But knowing and seeing were two different things. This was an actual, honest-to-goodness CROCO-DILE standing right in front of her. Trudy felt a little light-headed.

"That . . . ," she stammered, ". . . cannot be . . ."

"TRUDY!" Josh cried.

Trudy took a deep breath, working *very hard* to get control of herself. Then she nodded.

"Follow me," she said.

★

Josh was still anxious, but he didn't feel quite as alone now that he and Lyle had Trudy on their side. They followed her through the backstage area, which was crowded with performers and show staff. Most of the performers were too caught up in their own preparations to notice the crocodile running by.

The staff noticed. Big-time. PAs and stagehands dove out of the way left and right as Lyle passed. Being in show business meant keeping your cool no matter how weird things got. But this was beyond weird. Even for them.

A stage manager stood in the wings, listening to updates on his headset while scrolling through the show schedule.

"Kaysha from Kingsport, check," he responded to someone on the other end of the headset. He turned around to see whether his assistant had sent the first performer his way. "Where's Kaysha from—"

The words died in his throat as he saw Lyle standing in front of him. Josh was there, too, but the stage manager hardly noticed him. He was too busy goggling at the giant reptile towering over him.

"Security!" he squeaked into his headset. "We have a major problem!"

But security didn't respond. Nearby, Trudy grinned and held up a cord. It was the one connecting the stage manager's headset to his walkie-talkie so he could talk to the rest of the staff. Now it was dangling loose, connecting him with absolutely nothing at all.

The stage manager offered no resistance as Josh and Lyle hurried past him onto the side of the stage. Josh peered out from behind the curtain.

It was bright out there in the middle of the stage. *Really* bright.

Beyond the glare of the spotlight lay an ocean of faces. Right up front sat a panel of judges.

Josh looked up at Lyle. "You're just going to have to trust me now," he said. The two of them stepped past the curtain and emerged, blinking, onto the stage.

When Lyle came into view, there was a loud, sharp intake of breath throughout the audience. The judges' eyes widened. One of them leaped to his feet and fled from the building.

Lyle's shoulders slumped slightly. That was exactly the reaction he was dreading.

"This is it, Lyle," Josh whispered beside him. "You have to sing."

He turned the microphone stand toward Lyle. The theater was so quiet Lyle could hear the electric buzz of the lights overhead. The crowd was transfixed by the sight of the crocodile standing in front of the mic. They leaned forward in their seats, waiting to see what would happen next.

Lyle stood motionless, staring out at the audience. But he didn't see only their expectant faces. In his mind's eye, he heard the disappointed booing in Coney Island at his very first performance. He saw Hector's face falling as he realized Lyle still wouldn't sing at the investors' preview for their revival. Just like the people in front of him now, neither of those audiences had seen Lyle as a performer, the immense talent Hector had always claimed he was.

They hadn't seen anything special about him at all.

★

Josh watched from a few steps back, waiting for Lyle to sing. But Lyle stood rooted to the spot, not making a sound.

Suddenly Josh realized Lyle was shaking.

Josh's heart sank. His friend was absolutely petrified, beyond even what Josh had expected. He would do anything, no matter how terrifying it was, to save Lyle from being sent back to that zoo again. *Anything.*

Could he convince Lyle to face up to his greatest fear to save *himself*? Josh wasn't sure, but he knew he had to try.

He stepped forward. "We'll do it together," he told Lyle.

Lyle stared, uncomprehending, as Josh walked up to the mic and cleared his throat. Then he started to sing.

He sang the song Lyle and Hector had performed so many times on East 88th Street. Josh knew it by heart.

But that didn't mean he could sing it like they had. He already knew his own singing voice was kind of awful. Here, amplified and echoing through a huge Broadway theater in front of a capacity crowd, knowing that countless other Americans were tuning in on their TVs, phones, and computers at home, it sounded unimagin-ably, earth-shatteringly awful. Still Josh kept singing, plowing through the first verse on his way to the chorus. . . .

Lyle had always loved good music. What was coming out of Josh definitely wasn't that. But Lyle loved it just the same, maybe more. Josh was doing this for *him*. Sacrificing his dignity, his privacy, every ounce of self-respect he had. Lyle couldn't just see that. He could *feel* it.

Josh's eyes wandered to the aisles leading to the stage. Animal control officers were moving closer, tranquilizers drawn and eyes trained on Lyle.

But he couldn't think about that. He was all in, no matter what happened. He focused again on Lyle as he neared the chorus.

Lyle met his friend's eyes. He didn't see any fear in them. Instead he saw love and trust and courage. Plus-four strength courage, in fact, just like on that collector's card.

Josh had gifted Lyle that card. And now he was giving Lyle another gift: the gift of true friendship.

The kind a crocodile could rely on. The kind that gave him the confidence to believe he could do anything with this boy at his side.

Finally, Lyle began to sing. His voice was powerful, melodious, and utterly soaring. The microphone picked up the gloriously mellifluous notes and flung them throughout the theater.

The crowd stared. Jaws dropped from the judges' table to the orchestra seats to the last row of the mezzanine.

The crocodile sang his heart out, his voice growing stronger and more confident with every note. Before long the crowd leaped to its collective feet, loving every second of it. Even the animal control officers stopped where they were, mesmerized by what they were hearing.

Trudy was watching from the wings. Josh waved to her and the dance crew, who were waiting behind her. They all ran out onstage, accompanying Lyle's song with the most amazing dance moves Josh had ever seen.

The audience cried out in wonder, lifting their phones to film the whole thing. Lyle was in a world of his own, the world of the song. The music and lyrics built to a crescendo, rising higher and higher, until he threw back his head and belted out the last line.

A moment of silence and then it was the audience's turn to make some noise. They burst into a deafening roar of applause and cheered for Lyle in sheer delight! Lyle stared out at them. He was astonished and wondering and cautiously joyful all at the same time. Could it be true? No one was laughing at him. No one was scared. They liked him—they really, really *liked* him!

Mr. and Mrs. Primm scrambled into the back of the auditorium just in time to hear that last, soaring line. They were confused, but not for long. News of Lyle's triumphant performance, which had of course been beamed live across the country, was instantly the top story all over the *planet*. From Times Square to Timbuktu, people immediately flooded the internet with photos and videos of the singing crocodile and the tone-deaf kid who was his best friend.

Lyle and Josh didn't just break the internet. They smashed it into a zillion pieces. From Twitter to Sweep to the *New York Times* homepage, suddenly the duo was all anyone wanted to talk about. But in all that talk, there was nary a whisper about sending Lyle back to the zoo. Not anymore.

Josh's plan had worked—now everyone could see that Lyle was a very special crocodile indeed, an artist and a gentle soul who would not do harm to a flea.

Speaking of the zoo, Hector was still there. Still handcuffed to the wall. The guard's TV was tuned to *Show Us What You Got!*, which meant Hector and the guard, who had roused from his fall, had been able to watch the live performance. Hector's smile as he watched the crowd going wild was a little bit proud, a teensy touch envious—but mostly filled with vindication.

I knew he could do it! he thought.

★

In the theater, the audience clamored for an encore. Lyle and Josh were happy to comply. The music played on, with the entire crowd, judges included, on their feet dancing and singing along. Mr. and Mrs. Primm pushed their way forward, dancing and singing as well. Mr. Primm even pulled out his old wrestling whistle and added a rhythmic *toot-toot* to the percussion.

Maybe Josh would never be the wrestling champ his father had dreamed of, but that was okay. More than okay, actually. Mr. Primm was so proud of his strong, brave, one-in-a-million son that he felt as if he might burst.

★

Just about the only one who wasn't thrilled by Lyle's performance was Mr. Grumps. Like everyone else he saw the whole thing live. But he didn't cheer. He didn't dance along. He didn't even crack a smile. Loretta sat and watched, too, her eyes inscrutable as only a cat's eyes can be.

Even before the performance was over, Mr. Grumps started making phone calls. Then he spent the rest of the night pacing, grumbling, and glaring at nothing.

But not sleeping. No, he wouldn't rest until he took care of this . . . situation.

★

When the big day finally arrived, he was ready. He pulled out an ergonomic baby carrier he'd had specially customized to allow him to carry Loretta with him everywhere. Normally he took his time settling her in, making sure she was comfortable. But today he was too worked up to pay much attention. He shoved the cat into her carrier and hurried toward the subway, a glint of grim determination in his eyes. That ridiculous spectacle at the theater changed nothing. He'd worked too hard, too carefully, and now had the pieces in place. The time had come to finish the puzzle. Because yes indeed, he was very much intending to take care of this situation.

Once and for all.

New York City Housing Court was filled to overflowing. Journalists crowded the edges of the room, so eager for an interview that they sometimes ended up accidentally interviewing one another.

Josh looked around, amazed by everyone who had shown up to support his family. He spotted the wrestling coach from his school. The stage manager from *Show Us What You Got!* The paramedic who had tended to him at the zoo. Even two of the animal control officers who had subdued both him and Lyle back in their living room on East 88th Street. They caught Josh's eye and gave him a thumbs-up.

Trudy was there, too, of course. So were many of Josh's classmates. All of them were Lyle's superfans now.

Josh sat beside his mother. Directly in front of them, at one table facing the judge, sat Mr. Primm and Lyle. The other table was occupied by Mr. Grumps and an absolutely enormous pile of paperwork. Oh, and Loretta, who sat beside her owner looking bored.

"The point I'm making, your honor," Mr. Grumps said, his voice bristling with barely suppressed irritation, "is that *nothing has changed*."

He glanced over at Lyle with a frown. Lyle didn't notice. He was too busy sneakily drawing autographs for his fans with his tail.

"So the crocodile *sang*," Mr. Grumps continued loudly, with the distinct feeling that he didn't have anyone's full attention. "So what? It wasn't even that good. You're just impressed because it's a *crocodile*." Gathering steam, he thumped the pile of paperwork beside him. "But it was still broken out of the zoo, and according to every single one of the city's own regulations, it still *cannot* be kept in a domestic residence."

Lyle's army of fans turned their attention to

Mr. Grumps. A roar of protest rose all over the room.

"Order! Order!" The judge rapped his gavel. Then he looked at the Primms. "I'm afraid the plaintiff is right."

As Lyle's shoulders slumped, Josh's heart sank. He couldn't believe this. Despite everything that had happened, was Mr. Grumps going to win after all?

Suddenly a new voice rang out from the back of the room: "But who wants to be merely *right*?" Hector P. Valenti, star of stage and screen cried, stepping into the courtroom with a dramatic flourish.

Josh's eyes widened, and he traded a surprised look with Lyle. Hector strode forward, clutching a bundle of yellowed old documents under one arm.

"Yes, who wants to be right," he declared again, "when you can be *fabulously triumphant* instead?"

Nobody seemed to know quite what to make of that. People looked at one another in confusion. Mr. Grumps's jaw dropped in shock. Even the judge didn't make a sound.

Hector held up the papers. "Some documents, your honor, have come into my possession, which are of vital importance to this case," he said.

"What documents?" the judge asked.

"The original deed to the house on East Eighty-Eighth Street, for one," Hector replied.

Mr. Grumps gasped. "Wait, how did you get those papers?" he blurted out. "They were under my bed!"

"I was led to them." Hector grinned at him. "By a new friend."

Mr. Grumps followed Hector's gaze—right to Loretta. She looked up at her owner, knowing she was caught but not seeming to care very much.

"Let me see those," the judge said, waving a hand at Hector.

Hector handed the papers to a bailiff, who passed them to the judge. The judge studied them carefully.

"Those papers date from the time of my maternal grandmother, Evelyn T. Valenti," Hector explained. "She was not only the woman who built the house on East Eighty-Eighth Street, but also the woman who founded the zoo."

That caught Mr. Grumps's attention. As he turned to stare at the judge, Loretta sidled across the aisle toward Lyle and the Primms.

Mr. Grumps stared at her, devastated by her betrayal. Then he turned to the judge again as the full weight of what Hector had said settled in. Did he really think blabbing about some old relative was going to change anything?

"This is nonsense!" he exclaimed.

The judge was scanning one of the papers. "This is actually a special deed granted by the city of New York."

Hector nodded. "In acknowledgment of my grandmother's contributions to the city, and to accommodate her fascination with the animals that were rescued by her zoo."

The judge read aloud this time: "'The House on East Eighty-Eighth Street is hereby granted a special waiver to house any exotic creature as a pet.'"

Mr. Grumps leaped forward, ignoring court

protocol, and snatched the papers out of the judge's hand. He scanned them furiously.

"Your honor cannot be stupid enough to consider this," Mr. Grumps finally said. Some in the crowd murmured in shock.

The judge was silent for a long moment, studying Lyle and the Primms. Then he smiled.

"Approved!" he declared, banging his gavel.

The room erupted in cheers. Mr. Grumps felt his blood pressure shoot through the roof, incensed by the sheer, unadulterated injustice of it all.

He wouldn't have thought things could get any worse. That is, until he turned—and saw his beloved purebred Persian *cradled in Josh's arms*.

"Take your filthy paws off my Loretta!" he howled, lunging at the boy.

But he never reached him. Instead he felt the breath whooshing out of his lungs as he was slammed to the ground and pinned there in a magnificent half nelson.

His eyes swam, but he could still make out the face of Mr. Primm, All-State Champ '99, glaring down at him.

A day or two later, Josh was in the living room of the brownstone playing a hand-slap game with Lyle. Josh had a lot of experience at this game and won every time, though Lyle didn't seem to mind.

Mr. Primm hurried downstairs, dressed in shorts and a Hawaiian shirt. He dropped a suitcase by the front door next to several others, then blew his whistle.

Josh and Lyle traded a look. Josh loved how much more fun his dad was these days. But he kind of wished that Lyle hadn't reminded him about that whistle!

"Honey, we've got to go!" Mr. Primm called.

Hector shuffled in from the next room, looking disheveled in only a robe and slippers. "Wait. Go?" he said. "No one's going anywhere. I've already got Lyle over two hundred bookings in New York alone! Once we roll out a national tour we're going to be drowning in cash!"

Josh shook his head. "We're not going on a national tour. We're going on vacation."

"On . . . *what*?" Hector said.

Josh glanced over at his best friend. "Have you ever been on vacation before, Lyle?"

Lyle shook his head. Josh grinned.

"I got you a floatie!" he said.

Lyle gasped as Josh handed him an inflatable crocodile. He loved it! He refused to let go of it as the Primms went to work loading the suitcases into their car.

Soon the battered old station wagon was stuffed to the gills with bags, bikes, and beach paraphernalia. Hector stood on the curb watching as the family—including Lyle, of course, for he was part of the family—piled in and the car pulled away.

"Okay, fine!" Hector shouted after them. "We'll do a stadium tour instead! Fewer dates, but we'll pack in just as many people!"

The only responses were a honk of the horn

from Mr. Primm and waves from Josh and Lyle, who were leaning out either window in the back seat. The car slipped into the flow of traffic and soon disappeared around the corner, leaving Hector and his newly crushed dreams behind.

"Excuse me," a voice said.

Hector turned to see a girl standing there with a snake in a plastic terrarium. Hector gulped as he heard an ominous rattle from the end of the creature's tail.

"I'm sorry, kid, but—" Hector began.

"Do it, Malfoy," Trudy coached.

The rattlesnake shook its tail harder. It sounded a lot like a maraca. Then Malfoy began to beatbox, and the toe-tapping rhythm echoed down East 88th Street.

Hector was rooted to the spot, breathless with excitement as he bobbed his head to the snake's killer beat.

"Does he have an agent?" he demanded. When Trudy shook her head, Hector grinned, his plans for a certain singing crocodile drifting away—at least for the moment. "He does now!"

THE END